I0660254

CROSS OVER NINE

BOOKS IN THE ARGOSY LIBRARY:

UP JUMPED THE DEVIL
CLEVE F. ADAMS

THE BROTHERS OF THE SNAKE: THE
COMPLETE CHINATOWN CASES OF
JIMMY WENTWORTH, VOLUME 3
SIDNEY HERSCHEL SMALL

A CLUE TO THE COPPER: THE COMPLETE
CASES OF SILVER SKULL
RICHARD HOWELLS WATKINS

KINGDOM OF THE LOST: THE ADVENTURES
OF PETER THE BRAZEN, VOLUME 8
LORING BRENT

WORTH MILLIONS
RICHARD BARRY

TIGER DICK'S DOUBLOONS
DON MCGREW

PRESIDENTS: IMAGINARY MOMENTS IN
THE LIVES OF AMERICA'S GREAT
THEODORE ROSCOE

CROSS OVER NINE
MAX BRAND

ASOKA'S ALIBI: THE COMPLETE
ADVENTURES OF BEN QUORN, VOLUME 2
TALBOT MUNDY

THE LOST PUNCH: THE COMPLETE CASES
OF GILLIAN HAZELTINE, VOLUME 4
GEORGE F. WORTS

CROSS OVER NINE

MAX BRAND

ILLUSTRATED BY
JOSEPH A. FARREN

COVER BY
LEJAREN HILLER

POPULAR PUBLICATIONS · 2025

© 2025 Popular Publications, an imprint of Steeger Properties, LLC

First Edition—2025

PUBLISHING HISTORY

"Cross Over Nine" originally appeared in the July 7–August 11, 1934 issues of
   Detective Fiction Weekly magazine (Vol. 86, Nos. 1–6). Copyright © 1934 by The
   Frank A. Munsey Company. Copyright renewed © 1961 and assigned to
   Steeger Properties, LLC. All rights reserved.

ALL RIGHTS RESERVED

No part of this book may be reproduced or utilized in any form or by any means
   without permission in writing from the publisher.

Visit ARGOSYMAGAZINE.COM for more books like this.

CROSS OVER NINE

*Cherry Larue, the Idaho Gypsy; the Gaunt
Killer They Called "The Doctor"—Why
Are These Sinister Shadows Blocking
Witherby Away from the Man He
Had Crossed the World to Meet?*

1

THE TRAILING SHADOW

EVEN A GOOD tailor cannot keep a man's coat from hanging in folds about the shoulders, under the arms, across the breast. But there were no folds about the shoulders, under the arms, or across the breast of John Witherby. The coat fitted him as sleekly as it would have fitted a fat man. But he was not fat. His face was lean and hard and brown.

He was not very big. Certainly he was far from handsome. There was nothing about him to catch the eye, except the contrast between his gaunt face and the sleek of his coat; also, there was a triangular white scar at the base of his jaw, on the left side. The scar glistened when the jaw muscle worked in and out. People could not help looking at it.

Passengers were still pouring out of the train and red-caps on the run came up for the baggage; but John Witherby could not afford tips. At the bottom of the car steps he turned and called to the porter: "Throw it down."

"Throw it?" said the huge porter, hefting the weight of the bag in both hands. "You *mean* it?"

"Yeah. Throw it."

The porter bared his teeth with malice, heaved mightily, and with a groan of effort launched the suitcase into the air. Witherby, side-stepping, caught the handle and checked the fall with smooth ease.

The porter gasped. Then he ran down the steps and stared after his man. For he had flung down a leaden weight, but now Witherby was walking off with it as though it were packed with feathers. His body was hardly tilted to the side to balance the burden. There was a light spring in his step.

Men who lug dragging burdens keep their heads bowed and stare painfully at the ground, but the head of Witherby was high and unconcerned. In fact, he was pleased by a burden large enough to send a slight tingle through the nerves of his arm into the rubbery masses of strength that overlaid his shoulder. That was why he smiled a little, though the scene was far from pleasant. Sulphurous coal-smoke choked his nostrils, dark clouds of it rolled across the rafters of the trainshed.

The crowd streamed before him, heads bobbing up and down rapidly, out of step. He passed into the station. The

Witherby swung the weight of the table frame shoulder-high

lights reflected in the polish of the floor as deeply as in still water; outside there was the glow of the town and the sheen of the wet streets. Rain fell, small and soft.

"Where does a fellow get a bed for the night?" he asked a taxi driver.

"Community Lodging House," said the driver, carelessly. Then, after flashing a glance at Witherby, he felt that he might have made a mistake and added quickly: "Excuse me, sir. The Grand Hotel is the best place in town. Right up the street, there."

Witherby laughed, and walked on across the street. He had to move fast to avoid the traffic, but not so fast that he failed to see a man speak to the same taxi driver and then follow across the street.

Was he being trailed?

The charge split open the panels of the broken door

The only reason he was in this city was because he had received an urgent call from his granduncle, Daniel Finley, long a family legend for money and meanness. The letter had overtaken him, at last, in steaming Singapore. The letter had contained a command, no promises. But granduncle Daniel Finley had to die sometime; he had to leave his fortune to someone.

WITHERBY TOOK A zigzag course for six blocks. The fellow was still behind him, identified by a hat brim so extremely flexible that it jerked up and down in every gust of wind. And the blood of Witherby suddenly ran hot with happiness.

He turned into the first saloon, put his suitcase on the floor, and rested his left elbow on the edge of the bar. There were half a dozen others in the long room. Witherby got a glass of whisky. The image of it flashed a red streak in the mirror as he raised it to his lips. He took that color as a symbol. There was a promise of blood in the air. His jaw muscles worked for an instant. His eye gleamed.

And then, from the very tail of his eye, he saw the man of the fluttering hat brim come into the saloon. He was a wide-shouldered fellow, with a thick neck and a square face that seemed cushioned by nature to receive shocks.

He went over to a slot machine on the wall and got five cents' worth of peanuts. Then he came back to the bar and ordered a beer. He champed down a big mouthful of peanuts before he drank his beer. His way was to wash down the peanuts with a first mouthful. Then he poured down the whole glass, his neck swelling like a cobra's hood, vibrating with the pleasant effort.

Looking at this shadow, Witherby remembered for the

tenth time that he had no gun. But a gun gets a man into too much trouble. When a fellow is among darker races, from yellow to brown to black, gun trouble doesn't matter so much. But in the United States and Western Europe gun trouble is apt to be called "murder."

Witherby wanted almost passionately to do whatever anyone else would do, but he felt that he had better part himself from his gun before he landed. On the last night, with sad ceremony, he had dropped it over the rail. Afterwards he had felt very light, very naked. He felt naked again in the saloon, watching the gorilla who was trailing him.

If he had been in China, Japan, Mexico, or many other places, he might have guessed at a thousand important reasons why he should be followed; but for years he had not been in his native land. He was only twenty-five, but the five years he had been away from the States on this last trip seemed half a century to him. Why should he be trailed? Even if there were hidden grudges against him, who could recognize him in order to pay him out?

He went up the street again from the saloon.

Once he stopped to look into a lighted window and the man of the square face walked straight past him. When he went on, he was aware of the same form gliding out of the dark of an unlighted entrance and taking up the trail again.

He took a left turn to get back towards the brighter lights of the central town. Three men walked across the street, diagonally. They walked fast, but when they came onto his sidewalk they slowed their steps. They walked shoulder to shoulder, never looking back, but Witherby knew that they were thinking only of him. The shadow in his rear began to close up, taking very long strides. With-erby studied him with that quick backward glance which he had learned how to take through only the slightest turn of the head. A slant-eyed Chinaman had taught him that trick, away up north, in the frozen streets of Mukden.

It was a bad place. There were few inhabited houses. The fronts of them were shuttered. Their eyes were all out. They were as dead as statues. And there seemed to be hardly two street lamps to the block, throwing wavering streams of yellow over the pavement.

The buildings were shoulder to shoulder. There was no escape to either side.

He thought of springing upon a porch, flinging the suit-case through a window, and diving after it. But that would take time and he had four armed men against him.

They were four experts or they would not have been assigned to such a detail as this.

He was overtaking the three men ahead of him more rapidly. That simply meant that they were slowing down their steps, and the slowing of their gait meant that they were almost ready to strike.

He dropped to one knee and fumbled at a shoelace.

THE SQUARE-FACED FELLOW had been coming up so fast, rubber-shod for silence, that he could not check his pace instantly. He swung out as though to walk straight past the kneeling form. But the temptation of that bowed head was too great. Why should a job be left for four when one man can finish it?

At the same moment, kneeling John Witherby saw the three men ahead of him turn in unison; and he also saw the flash of the shadow's gun.

He reached for that flash with a long arm. His fingers closed on the warmed steel of the automatic. He pulled the gun out of the frantic grasp of the shadow, as one might pull a toy out of the soft hand of a baby, and the shadow lurched towards him, off balance. Witherby took him by the shoulders and faced him towards the three.

Two of them were half crouched over their guns. One had dropped to his knee to sight more carefully. Witherby heard and felt the shock of the three big bullets as they hit the body of the shadow. It was the work of experts, right enough.

The fellow shrieked once and was still. He hung limp in the grasp of Witherby, like a loosely stuffed scarecrow.

It was the scream that routed the three ahead. They wavered. The man who had dropped to one knee used that posture like a sprinter to make a fast start, and fled; the others followed.

Witherby dropped the limp man like a sack. He heard the man's head bump loudly on the pavement. Then he tried his hand at the fugitives. The leader ran like a flying snipe. The sporting blood of Witherby rose. It was only at the shifting, dodging, bent form that he fired, three times. At the third shot the man leaped into the air. He ran on around the corner with his arms flung high above his head.

They were out of sight, all three of them, now. But still the rapid beating of their feet drifted back to the ear of Witherby. The sounds faded.

He looked up and down the street.

Not a window, not a door had opened. Not a soul had appeared, drawn by the noise of screams and gunshots.

He kneeled by the loose form on the pavement. The man

was dead. His mouth hung open. His eyes stared horribly. So Witherby closed the lids.

He reached inside the coat and pulled out a thin sheaf of letters and a wallet. There was money in the wallet, a good, thick wad of greenbacks. A man of great delicacy would not have touched this cash, perhaps, but Witherby was not a man of great delicacy. He had been fishing in waters troubled by sharks most of his life.

He put the money in his vest pocket, the letters inside his coat, picked up the suitcase, and went on exactly as before. The only difference was that he carried the bag in his left hand now. His right hand might be needed at any moment for a hurried trip to his hip pocket.

The weight of the gun comforted him. He no longer felt naked.

2

A GOOD TOWN

WITHERBY WAS LESS directly headed for the home of his granduncle, Mr. Daniel Finley.

Previously he had had eight dollars and some eleven cents in his pocket. Now he had an unknown sum, whose weight was far heavier in the thoughts of Witherby than the memory of the dead man he left behind him. Another fellow of conscience and tender heart might have rushed at once to warn the police and call for an ambulance. But Witherby stopped at the nearest saloon, entered its family room, dropped his ponderous suitcase on one chair, his hat on a second, and sat down himself on a third. He made a small thunder by whacking the flat of his hand on the top of the round table, whose varnish had been faded in round spots by the liquors which had dripped on it.

"Whisky!" said Witherby, when the bartender stuck his head through the door.

The head remained stuck there for a moment. It was closely cropped. The pallor of the scalp helped to make the blond hair blonder. But the top of the head was very small, like a little white cap set on top of the immense red face. Wrinkles of flesh extended from the neck almost to the top of the cropped head. After a long moment of observation the bartender removed his head from the doorway.

Witherby had time to count the money from the dead man's wallet. It was even more than he had hoped. There were ten twenties in a solid wad. Behind them were five fifties. Behind the fifties were three five-hundred dollar bills.

"Two thousand dollars, almost, in that gorilla's paw," said Mr. Witherby, softly. He put the money back in his vest pocket. His entire attitude towards life was changed by the possession of such a sum. He felt lifted to a height. Granduncle Daniel Finley was a thought far removed. Much, much ground should be covered before ever he saw Granduncle Daniel.

He pulled out the letters he had taken and went through them. Three letters, one a bill, one from a girl, one from a friend. All three cast some light on the character of the dead man. He was addressed on all the envelopes as Mr. Samuel Miller.

The bill was from a landlord, pointing out that Mr. Miller was five months in arrears with his rent.

The letter from the girl ran:

> DEAR DUTCH:
>
> I seen Mamie Truman the other day. She says she seen you with Myrtle, that blond fluzie, over on Chatham Street. Honest, Dutch, when I heard that I gagged. You must of been drunk. You can spread yourself pretty thin, but don't try to cover too much. Come around and tell me what you can see in that carrot-topped mug of Myrtle.
>
> Always loving you just the same.
>
> > Yours sincerely,
> >
> > SYLVIA.

Mr. Witherby lighted Sylvia's letter and watched it blaze until a puff of white, acrid smoke hung in the air and some shreds of black carbon and of gray ash descended to the floor.

The third letter was more interesting. It ran:

DEAR DUTCH:

Play everything close to your chest. Even if you cleaned up the other day, sit tight and take the stuff that's being handed out. I seen the Doctor. He's got a job for you and me and Mark and Slip. There's a coupla hundred bucks apiece in it and all we do is rub out a guy with no friends in town.

Come around and see me soon.

LEFTY.

The man who had dropped to one knee had used his gun in the left hand; he was the fellow who had run dodging, like a snipe; he was the one the bullet had hit before he got out of view around the corner.

Witherby lighted the second letter. The smoke of it was rising, the flaming body of the paper was falling slowly towards the floor when the bartender came in, carrying the glass of whisky and a water chaser on a small, round tray.

He came up and put down the drink. He set his foot on the last of the flame.

"What are you? A damn firebug?" asked the barman. "Or some other kind of a nut?"

WITHERBY LOOKED ON the man with approval that lighted his eyes and almost made him smile. The ample thickness and breadth of the crop-head was overlaid with fat, but there was plenty of man beneath the fat.

"You don't like my looks, do you?" asked Witherby.

"Not a damn bit," said the bartender, with flaring nostrils and gleaming little eyes, like those of a pig.

"Shake on the idea, then," suggested Witherby, holding out his hand.

"Sure—I'll shake hands on anything," said the barman, and stuck out a great mitt.

Witherby gripped it briefly, released it. The barman stood with slow waves of pain wrinkling his face, staring down at his hand. The ends of his fingers were pale purple. The center of his hand was white. The whole hand was stiff, crumpled, lifeless.

"Busy in there, George?" asked Witherby.

"No," said the bartender, in a changed voice.

"Get yourself a drink and come back here and sit down."

The bartender got himself a tall whisky, returned, and sat down. His little pig-eyes were opened round. They were the palest China-blue.

"You don't look it," he said to Witherby. "I wouldn't of ever guessed it."

He began to rub his injured right hand, softly.

"What sort of a town is this?" asked Witherby.

"Wide open."

"Who runs it?"

"A lot of friendly guys."

"Is the Doctor one of them?"

The bartender half rose from his chair. Sitting down again, slowly, he first glanced quickly over his shoulder. Then he tossed off his whisky at a swallow.

"Him!" he said. "You being sent to him?"

"I need to see him," said Witherby.

"Will he need to see you?"

"So bad he's been spending money to find me."

"Why don't you go to him, then?"

"My steer only got me as far as this town. I don't know where the Doctor hangs out. I never saw his face."

"Wait a minute," said the bartender. "I'll go telephone. What's your name?"

"Smith."

"John Smith, eh?"

"No, Jack," said Witherby.

The bartender grinned and retreated through the doorway. He closed the door behind him, but Witherby, his ear pressed to a wide crack, could just make out the subdued voice that was presently speaking.

"Hello, chief? There's a bozo here that says the Doctor wants to see him. He don't know the way. It don't make no difference to me, but it might make a lot of difference to the Doctor. He don't look so much, but he *is* much. He's a Sandow or something, and he's as smooth as a seal. I ain't telling you. I'm asking you. Come on down and give him the once-over for yourself. All right, then. I'll tell him. So long."

The bartender returned to find Witherby back in his chair sipping the whisky in small swallows, as though he loved the smoke and fire of the drink.

"You'll find the Doctor over at his own dump. That's 112 East Fifteenth Street."

"How do I know the Doctor?"

"By the jaw on him. You could get a double hand-hold on his chin."

"Thanks," said Witherby. "Fill 'em up."

The bartender brought in a bottle. Witherby took it from his hand, filled the barman's glass, and then put the mouth of the bottle to his lips. There it remained tilted for some moments. When he restored the bottle to the table the barman looked straight into the eyes of "Jack Smith" and saw that the eyes were clean, clear, and untroubled. The bartender sighed; he knew the dynamite qualities of that whisky. He picked up the twenty that was slipped onto the table and made change from his pocket. Witherby picked up fifteen and left the rest.

"This is a good town," said Witherby. "I'm going to like it."

"Yeah, as far as it goes. Maybe there won't be enough of it for you," said the barman.

Witherby waved his hand and went onto the street.

3

TEN SECONDS TO LIVE

HE PICKED UP a taxi that slid him through the center of the town until he stopped it at the Ridgeview Hotel. Some hotels have international faces. The Ridgeview was one of them. By the look of it, Witherby knew instantly the ratty lobby he would find inside, the chambermaids with soiled aprons, the yellow face of the desk clerk, the worn carpets, the smell of must and of stale food in the air.

He paid the cab and carried his suitcase inside. It was just the interior that he had imagined. In places of this ilk the comings and goings of clients were hardly noted. The top floor was the eighth. He had found it handy, very often, to be near the roof, so he took a room on that floor. He got the cheapest room they could give him, partly because he wanted to be in the quiet of the rear of the building. He liked modern cities well enough, and he had seen most of them, but his brain worked better in silences like those of the desert—or the jungle.

When he got to his room he leaned out the window and looked down the steep wall into the small backyards, paved with concrete. One who dived from this height would splash when he landed. He looked up and saw that by standing on the sill of the window he could reach the projecting eaves.

He could not tell when he would need to reach those eaves. All he knew was that in this town a mysterious power called "The Doctor" had hired four thugs to put him out of the way and posted spies at the railroad depot to mark him down when he entered the place.

How could the Doctor have learned a description of him?

What earthly purpose could the Doctor have in mind?

Instead of proceeding at once to the house of his grand-uncle, it was the fixed purpose of John Witherby to find the Doctor and check the growing menace at its roots.

He was humming when he put his suitcase on the bed and opened it. He laid out in the drawers of his bureau a hard-bosomed shirt, two suits, besides a dinner jacket he hung in the closet. He arranged the rest of his apparel with the neatness and speed of the habitual traveler.

There were some odd items remaining. One was a Bible, that thick Reader's Bible of Moulton. There was an equally thumb-worn one-volume Shakespeare. This library he put on the small table beside his bed.

In a small top drawer of the bureau he stowed away a flat-handled knife with a six-inch blade covered by a shagreen case. There was a complete sewing kit in a canvas cover-all, a small medical kit with sharp lancets and a number of drugs, a sand-bag harnessed to a strong elastic wristband, and some oversoles of a composition softer than rubber and not so apt to slip on wet going. All around the sides of the suitcase was worked a forty-foot length of rawhide rope, heavy as quicksilver and almost as flexible.

Only over this implement did he linger for a moment, making the slender length of it twist into some odd, airy figures before he slumped it in a heap into a drawer.

Then he stripped and, since he had no bathroom, stood at the wash basin and scrubbed himself thoroughly, and then shaved. When he stood motionless he looked soft from head to foot, but at the least movement little snakes of muscle writhed through the apparent softness. When at last he yawned and stretched himself, his whole body leaped into a quivering life of its own. The big muscles that flowed over his shoulders seemed to have their rootage in the small of his back. He was brown as a Mexican, except for the single curving white mark that ran up over his hips and the small of his back. It looked as though he had been wearing a loincloth. But where would a white man do that except in far, southern seas?

After he had rubbed himself dry, he did a few exercises and stood at last on one hand, easing his weight up and down on the single arm until even those rubbery muscles turned hard and then began to shudder. When he threw himself back on his feet he was in a fine glow, and he dressed rapidly.

Somewhere in that rainy night, Mark and Slip were talking about the killing of Dutch, the wounding of Lefty. Perhaps the Doctor himself was organizing his forces for the further attack on Witherby.

What was the meaning of it all? It was as foolish to ask that as to demand of beasts of prey why they hunt for raw meat.

HE PUT ON a thin raincoat. It was seven blocks to 112 East Fifteenth Street, and he walked the distance. He was very dry. He stopped twice for whisky. The liquor began to knock at his brain a little. He was aware of a slight thickening of the upper lip, but he laughed at the symptoms. His head had to be at least as hard as his hands. Otherwise it would have gone to pieces with hard usage long ago.

One hundred and twelve East Fifteenth Street was a corner building, with a restaurant on the ground floor. The restaurant windows were curtained with white silk. The light struck a rosy glow through it. Windows like that meant high prices.

Beside the restaurant there was another entrance to the building. Witherby rang the bell there, and a uniformed porter opened the door. He had a paper-white face, a square, resolute face set in lines so hard that he seemed to be enduring great pain.

"I've got an appointment with the Doctor," said Witherby.

The porter stepped back, slowly. It could not be said that he was reluctant about letting the stranger enter, but Witherby was aware of the keen sidelong glance which studied him in detail. He entered a wide hall. Chairs stood on each side of the center rug. Smoking stands were beside the chairs. The hall had been turned into a lobby.

The porter disappeared through a doorway. He came back after a moment.

"Somebody telephoned you were coming?" he asked.

"That's right."

"Come on up," said the porter, and went to the elevator in the corner of the hall. "For the chief," he said to the elevator boy.

"Boy" was only a term, not a fact. This fellow in the elevator had a scarred face, and the scars looked like knifecuts to the expert eye of Witherby. It was plain that the Doctor kept only chosen specimens about him.

"Second floor on the left," said the elevator boy.

Witherby tapped on that door. He noticed that the hallway was like that of a dwelling, with rugs on the floor, pictures on the wall, a small table here and there and two or three floor lamps. When he heard a voice call inside the room he pushed the door open and went inside. He carried the automatic a little higher than his hip as he walked in.

He thought, at first, that he had stepped into a lady's boudoir. There were curtains tied back with ribbons, and bright pictures on the walls, and slender-legged chairs, and a Persian rug with a pinetree pattern worked through it. A thin, long, light man reclined on a davenport against a heap of cushions, with his hands clasped behind his head. He had such a chin that Witherby could have laid hold on it with both hands. The narrowness of his face and the extreme brightness of his eyes was what took the mind of Witherby.

Now those bright eyes paid no heed to the levelled gun.

"Glad to see you, Witherby," he said.

"I'll bet you are," answered Witherby, locking the door behind him with his left hand.

"Lock the other doors, too," suggested the Doctor.

"I will," said Witherby. There were three other doors. He locked them one by one. The Doctor kept a faint smile on his lips, but that smile might be no more than a sham. Some men try to prove their indifference by inviting disaster closer.

"Sit down," said the Doctor.

"Thanks," said Witherby.

He took one of the soft-cushioned, spindle-legged chairs. The automatic rested across his knee. With his left hand he opened a little figured lacquer box on a table beside him and took out a cigarette. He took a lighter from the same table and flicked on the flame. When he was smoking he sighed a little.

"It's too easy, eh?" said the Doctor.

"Why do they call you the Doctor?" asked Witherby.

"Because my operations are almost always successful."

"Why did you start to operate on me?"

"Call it an instinct."

"Mugs like Dutch and Lefty and Mark and Slip can never hang me up."

"Your bartender friend talked freely, did he?"

"That flat-head? Don't blame him. He didn't talk at all, except over the telephone."

"How did you become intimate with him? So quickly, I mean. An old shipmate."

"A good guy like me knows how to make friends fast," said Witherby. "What put you on my trail, Doctor?"

"The thing that men like you and me should do is to look forward, not back," answered the Doctor.

"You don't want to talk?"

"I want nothing more. And I want you to hear."

"Doctor," said Witherby, "you're going to look as far forward as hell unless you open up and tell me exactly who put you on my trail."

"YOU WOULDN'T DO that!" said the Doctor.

"I wouldn't bump you off?" echoed Witherby. "Not after you've put your thugs on me?"

"I mean shooting—in a place like this!" said the Doctor. "You're not going to disappoint me that way, are you? Not after building up my expectations!"

"You kind of make me feel sorry for you," said Witherby, grinning. "Why shouldn't you stretch out and turn stiff in this place as well as the next one?"

"Because there are men over us and under us and beside us, and the crack of a gun would bring them in here. Locked doors wouldn't stop them."

"If I couldn't stop them from coming in, perhaps they couldn't stop me from going out."

"I see how it is," said the Doctor. He sat up, slowly, and with his elbows clasped against his ribs, folded his hands over his chin. The upper part of his face was no larger than that of a boy. The small eyes twinkled almost with merriment.

"Strong and confident in your strength, like the ox," said the Doctor. "And, like the ox, you'll die young, Witherby. However, you're not such a fool as you seem. You've taken heed of my words."

He stood up.

"Sit down again," said Witherby.

"Do you really think that I'm afraid of you?" asked the Doctor. He walked straight forward and reached a hand, slowly, toward the automatic. Witherby caught that extended hand.

"You poor fool!" he said. "I ought to salt you away, for this."

"Stop smashing my arm," said the Doctor.

He backed away, as Witherby released him. "You shook hands with the bartender, did you?" he suggested. Witherby only grinned at him, and the Doctor began to massage his bruised arm with much tenderness.

"I think I could use you. I know that you could use me," said the Doctor.

"I can use you for some information," answered Witherby. "Open up and talk, Doctor. Tell me who put you on my trail."

"Confidences," said the Doctor, "are things that I never betray. If I had in mind a good, convincing lie I'd tell it to you. But since I haven't one in time I simply inform you that I shall not give you the information."

"If you're interested in God Almighty say your last words to Him," said Witherby.

"Going to shoot?"

"In ten seconds, brother, I'm going to open your way to a better life."

"You don't alarm me," said the Doctor. "I'll count the ten for you."

And he did so, slowly, with a smile. When he reached ten the gun of Witherby did not speak.

4

THE DOCTOR OF DEATH

JOHN WITHERBY STRAIGHTENED in his chair and nodded.

"You have a good, steady nerve," he said.

"Not a bit. I'm very nervous, in fact. But you're not a murderer, Witherby. Besides, you had a chance to see some of my men on your way up, and you knew that to get out would be a hard job."

"I'll have to surprise you," said Witherby.

"Try to."

"I came here to blow hell out of you."

He got up and walked to the Doctor.

"It makes too much noise," said the Doctor.

Witherby gathered in one swift hand the lapels of the Doctor's coat.

"I could strangle you in one minute or break your neck in three seconds," he suggested.

"Shooting might be execution. Strangling would be murder."

"By what code?"

"By your code," said the Doctor.

"Not by yours, damn you!" snarled Witherby.

"No, not by mine. Poison or a gun or a slungshot, or anything. When I determine on results, I usually get them."

"By God, I owe it to the world. I ought to break you in two, right now."

"You won't do that."

"No, I don't suppose I will, but I ought to."

He stepped slowly back from the Doctor. "I'm glad the melodrama is ended," said the Doctor. "Now we can talk and make a little headway."

"All right," said Witherby. "I'll waste a few moments on you."

"You're going to waste long and happy years with me," said the Doctor.

"At how much a week?" grinned Witherby.

"Two hundred dollars—for a start."

Witherby blinked. He thought of forty or fifty dollars a month on the Western range; or three dollars a day in the bitter harvest fields, shoveling coal in the bowels of a ship; swinging a twelve-pound sledge all day long; slaving in the hot deeps of a mine—he thought of a hundred pictures of himself at work. There had been adventure that paid more, to be sure. In the South Seas there are a great many things that a man can do.

"You're about twenty-eight years old," said the Doctor.

"Twenty-four."

"Really? Well, you've lived your years. Things will be easier for you when you commence with me."

"What sort of work, doctor?"

"Easy work, I tell you. Taking care of me, for one thing. I've always wanted a 'secretary' like you."

"There's only one thing I'll do with you."

"What's that?"

"Walk downstairs with you as far as the street."

"Are you sure?"

"Dead sure. I'm not killing you, Doctor, but I'd rather murder you than work for you."

"I'm not entirely surprised," said the Doctor, nodding. "I wish that you could spend some more time thinking this over, but I see that you're a fellow who only thinks once on each subject. I'm to be your bodyguard as far as the street, eh? Come on, then."

He went straight to that door of the room through which Witherby had entered, and which he had locked behind him. Taking hold of the knob, the Doctor opened the door at once. While Witherby was in the room some agency must have slipped the bolt from the hall, soundlessly. He had the stubnosed automatic in his pocket, now, while he stood close to the Doctor's back.

His other hand gripped the arm of the man while the Doctor opened the door very slowly, and when it was wide moved a quarter-step forward and shook his head solemnly.

The reason for that signal was apparent by the time Witherby had stepped out into the hall in his turn. For a man was retreating from either side of the door, another fellow was sitting down in a chair a short distance away, and a fourth, near the elevator, was hastily hiding some bright, metal object under his coat.

"Looks as though we might have had company in there," said Witherby to the Doctor.

"Fools are always breaking in," said the Doctor. He said it loudly, looking up and down the hall, but the four looked back at him with set, immobile faces.

Murder was in every one of them. The air of the place reeked with murder. The soft carpet whispered under the feet of Witherby only one word, and the faint smile on the pale face of the Doctor seemed to be printed there for the same effect.

AS THEY WENT to the elevator, a chill worked up and down between Witherby's shoulder blades. He was glad when he could step into the elevator and glide down with it to the ground floor.

The lobby which had been empty when Witherby arrived had five men in it now. They lounged here and there, appearing indifferent, but with bright, deadly side glances they studied the face of Witherby as he came out behind the Doctor.

"More of your helpers, eh?" said Witherby.

"Sometimes one has almost too many friends," said the Doctor, with his smile; he walked slowly, with a long, stalking stride, to the street.

The rain was still falling, but in a very fine mist. The light of the city struck upwards into it, like fire into rolling clouds of smoke. The sounds of traffic came mournfully and from far away to the ear of Witherby. The street before him was empty, polished with water, streaked by thin reflections.

"And so we must part, my friend?" said the Doctor. "That's a regret to me."

"Why do you talk in this damned, hypocritical, whining way?" asked Witherby. "Do you think I've forgotten the way Dutch died?"

"I'm sure you haven't," said the Doctor, "and neither have

I. But it's better to have such things in mind—when we meet again, Witherby. Don't you think so?"

His voice remained caressing. But his eyes blazed as he went on in the same gentle tone: "You've walked into this place against my will, and you've walked out of it a free man. You've lowered me in the eyes of every one of my men. I'm a certain vital percentage smaller today than I was yesterday. I lead a pack that's accustomed to see me strike home every time I show my teeth. How much harm you've done me I don't know. Enough to make it necessary for you to die, Witherby. Be assured of that. You have not many days. Perhaps you have not many hours."

Witherby, looking over his shoulder at the long, pallid ugliness of that face and the terrible brightness of the eyes, stepped off down the street with no more words of farewell. The Doctor made no signal to his men. He simply remained in the doorway with the fine rain descending about him until Witherby turned a corner and shut out the nightmare.

A cruising taxicab passed. He hailed it and said to the driver: "Take me some place where the lights never go out." Then he sat back against the cushions and set his teeth hard. He could not keep out of his mind the conviction that the Doctor knew of what he spoke. Death might be riding invisible beside him at this moment.

5

THE ROOM UPSTAIRS

GREAT ELECTRIC LETTERS spelled the word *"Kelcy's."*

"This oughta be your medicine, chief," said the taxi driver.

"Noise, and a lot of people making it," said Witherby.

"There's nothing else but," said the driver. So Witherby went inside.

The tremor of the jazz band was in the air of the hall; the voice of it droned thin in the anteroom where he checked his hat; and when he came out into the main room he found exactly what he had wanted—a huge place, a dazzle of lights, with cigarette smoke going up in clouds.

It was exactly what he wanted for several reasons. In the first place, he would find safety in the crowd. Even the long arm of the Doctor would not reach him here; even the Doctor's killers would not be hired for a slaughter in such a public place as this. The second important reason was that he wanted to enjoy uninterrupted quiet; and the greatest solitude is that which a man finds in the middle of a crowd.

He managed to find a corner table where he could put his back against the wall and keep the entire spread of the picture constantly before his face. He ordered whisky, straight, and tipped a waiter a dollar to see that the glass was never empty. After that, he forgot the world about him as well as he could—as well as a lion forgets the jungle in which it crouches.

After a time he took out a pencil and began to draw vague designs on the table cloth, parallel lines and small circles, exactly tangent. The moment those circles ceased being exactly in touch with the lines, and overlapped or failed to meet the straight strokes, he would be drunk. He would be drunk, but still capable of walking and talking—still capable of putting two packs of playing cards together and then tearing them across, in one vast, finger-numbing effort.

Time ceased for him.

There was some reason of profound importance behind the Doctor's desire to get him out of the way. He felt that he had to find that reason. There could be only one—that the Doctor wished to prevent him from getting to old granduncle Daniel Finley. But why should he wish to do that? What possible interest could the Doctor have in the miserly farmer?

Now and then the glass of red-brown liquor rose to the lips of Witherby. Now and then he took a deep breath. Otherwise his only movements were with his pencil.

The night was sliding past him with wonderful velocity. Still the pencil drew meaningless diagrams on the white cloth.

The second fresh table cloth was before him, and it was being filled with the same symbols—the straight lines meeting one another at varying angles and all exactly tangent to neat circles, big and small. His mind worked better when his eye was occupied in this manner.

The air grew more stale, thicker with smoke. When new arrivals entered in the early hours of the morning they brought a thin wedge of fresh air in with them.

The dancing had paused for a spell of entertaining. And the singing voice of a girl cut through the outer barriers of his absent-mindedness, penetrated the donjon-keep of his inner mind. He looked out and was aware for the first time in real hours of what was going on about him.

Across the smoke he could see the singer on the stage in front of the orchestra. The words of the song were still making their way in his mind. They were not bawdy; they were not love; they were not "blues"; they were simply songs of the gipsy trail.

She was a dark girl. She had black hair and black eyes. He knew even in the distance that those eyes were black.

She had a béret pushed back on her curly head; She smiled as she sang; instead of taking breath in the pauses she was laughing; she was laughing because the joy of the gipsy trail kept bursting out of her.

When she ended the audience stood up for her and yelled. The musicians stood up and clapped. The drummer beat a roll for her honor.

"Who is she?" Witherby could hear all voices asking.

"What's that?" he asked the waiter.

"It's a new one on me," said the waiter. "Kelcy's always got something new up his sleeve."

"Go get her. I want her to have a drink with me," said Witherby.

"They're calling her back," said the waiter.

The yelling of the crowd and the stamping died out. The

girl had come back. She was not on the orchestra's stage now, but walking about among the tables.

"Don't bother her," said Witherby to the waiter. "She's going to come here to my table."

"Did you high-sign her?"

"No, but a spark jumped."

"You're one of them that know, eh?" said the waiter, grinning.

THE GIRL, IN fact, came straight to the table of Witherby. She seemed to be passing; and then she paused, she turned back, she sang straight at him.

In a time like that he always took note of small things. She was dressed for the street. There was nothing gipsy about her clothes except for the bright crimson sash that girdled her, and something in her way of wearing the beret at that absurd angle. Even her skin was not swarthy. It was only olive, with a rich color worked into it.

She was not beautiful. She was something better. A ripple of life flowed through her; a breath of life came out of her. She carried into the stale air of the café the freshness of those outer spaces about which she was singing.

So she sang her song straight through and kept her eyes on Witherby.

When she ended he spoke. But she was turning away already. She was singing her way back to the stage, and never pausing at another table. She was on the stage. She was vanishing from it. And the place was bellowing for yet another encore.

"You knew she'd come, all right," said the waiter. "But she ain't the kind to sit down at a table and take a drink."

"Why not?" asked Witherby.

"I dunno," said the waiter. "I've served a hundred thousand of 'em, and now and then you find a lady."

"Get on the heels of that lady and tell her that I want to see her. Wait a minute."

He drew another straight line; he made a circle beside it and the circle missed the line by a small but vital margin.

"I don't know," muttered Witherby. "But—yes—go tell her what I said."

The waiter went, shrugging his shoulders on the way. He came back presently, with an air of surprise.

"She'll see you," he said. "Not in here, though. One of the private dining rooms upstairs. She'll see you there."

Witherby stood up. He could feel the liquor in his upper lip, in the big arteries of his throat, and in his knees.

"How far from morning?" he asked.

"The dawn's starting," said the waiter.

Witherby paid his bill and followed the waiter out of the big room, up a flight of stairs, and down a narrow hall. An end-door opened on a little square room with a white-covered table in the center of it; he could see a sparkle of glass, and chairs with red velvet cushions drawn up against the wall, like luxurious little sinners.

The girl sat in a corner, polishing her fingernails against the heel of her other hand. She gave the nails a last look before she stood up to meet Witherby. The crimson sash was gone. Instead of the béret she wore a hat that covered a good bit of her brow. Her face seemed smaller, therefore. The whole effect was smaller. There was only the eyes and the smile to recall the figure which had dominated the big-crowded room downstairs.

Witherby shook hands with her. He asked what she drank.

"A slice of lemon in soda water," she told him.

"Quit it," said Witherby. "A slice of lemon in gin, you mean."

"Soda," said the girl.

He looked at her a little darkly, ordered her drink, whisky for himself. Then he sat her down at the table.

She put her elbows on the edge of it, interlaced her fingers under her chin, and smiled for him. The waiter came in with whisky. He left again. She was sipping her sparkling water, with the green gold of a lemon slice floating awry in the glass.

"Somewhere they're sure to have your name spelled out in electric lights, but I haven't seen it," said he.

"Cherry Larue is my name," she answered, "and it's never been anything big, not even a check."

"Cherry is a swell name," said Witherby.

"That's why they gave it to me," said the girl. "It's the only thing parents can give a child without spending money."

"They spent money on you," said Witherby. "Larue—that sounds French."

"French from Iowa," she answered.

"Are you from the boulevards of Des Moines?"

"I'm from out that way."

"Cherry Larue is a pretty nice name," said Witherby. "Let me put some whisky in that water."

"No," she said.

"Don't you drink?"

"With meals."

"We'll eat," said he.

"Let's talk," said the girl. "Or do you have to keep on slogging yourself with that whisky?"

"Never mind about me. Smoke?"

"I don't smoke."

"Stop it, will you?" begged Witherby. "And I thought you were a real gipsy, and all that!"

"You know how it is," said the girl. "I have to take care of myself. Yellow fingers are not so good, either. And soiled goods go down to the basement onto a bargain counter."

"You figure things out, eh?"

"Sure. I have to. I haven't much face to go on."

"It's what I like," said Witherby.

"Make you feel at home, eh?"

"It's only when you sober up and then look down that the Indian comes out of you."

"That's right," she replied. "I have to be one of those damned, highheaded beauties. If my chin isn't pointing at the north star, I'm no picture. I wish I had a restful face. One of the up-and-sidewise lookers. What an easy time they have of it, sinking their chins into their fur collars and being coy or sulking a little. I never have a chance at that line. When your chin is in the air you've got to smile or be damned."

"You'll make your way in the world," he told her.

It's hard work," she answered. "The sitting and looking girls have everything easy."

"They get fat and then where are they? You keep to your song and dance and you'll still be gathering the long green when the rest of 'em are back in kitchen mechanics. Give me your hand."

She put her right hand on the table. He turned it palm up.

"Give me your other hand." She let him have it. "Lots of tennis and golf, and plenty of riding, too," said he. "Cherry, what made you dig into the dirty night life? You've been raised like a lady."

SHE TRIED TO jerk her hands away. He held them in one of his, lightly. She struggled until he increased his pressure ever so little. Then she caught her breath and sat perfectly still. Fear widened her eyes and polished them with brightness.

He released her hands, instantly, smiling.

He picked up the whisky bottle which he had made the waiter bring and filled his glass once more. "Are you going to slug yourself with some more of that stuff?" she asked.

"It's only scratching the surface," he told her. "Loosen up and tell John Witherby the truth about yourself."

"What truth?" she asked.

"Why you happen to be sitting here and talking to him."

"Because you weren't like the others. You were sitting alone, drinking by yourself, making marks on the cloth. I was curious."

"Is that the whole reason you came up here?"

"Yes."

"It sounds a little fishy. But if you're a lady, Cherry, you can't tell a lie. Go on and talk about yourself."

He swallowed half his glass of whisky. The sour of it spread through the roof of his mouth to his very eyes; the burn of it reached his stomach and his brain.

"If I tell that story it will take a long time."

"I've got plenty of time."

"Well, I'll have to telephone first."

"Go ahead. I'll be waiting here."

She went to the door of the room, turned, looked back at him with a hesitant air. Then she went on out. Something she had wanted to say had died in her throat.

He finished his glass of whisky and drank another, slowly. He had enough of the stuff in him to have knocked out a pair of ordinary men, but he was merely breathing a little hard.

After a time he realized that the girl had been away for a long period. He went to the window, drew the curtains, raised the sash, pushed the shutters open. The gray, wet air of the dawn pushed in against him. He saw the city dimly receding through the rain and suddenly knew that Cherry Larue was not coming back to him at all.

"I've got a mind to wreck this joint," said he to himself.

He went to the door and jerked it open. The hall was dark. The dawn which filled the room could soak only a short distance into the blackness, but it went far enough to show him figures in the gloom, and one man standing with his arm outstretched and a trembling gleam of metal in his hand.

The gun spattered fire and thunder.

Witherby leaped back and slammed and locked the door. Bullets were snipping through it and thudding against the opposite wall.

6

THE ATTACK

THE WET BREATH of the dawn that poured through the open window came in irregular gusts. The mist was visible in the electric light. It was like the foretaste of death. The cold of it worked a chill into the heart of Witherby.

No, it was not merely the gray hour, and the cold. It was the knowledge that the girl had been used to bait and trap him.

The Doctor—it was the Doctor who was behind all this.

He jumped to the window. Four stories of shuttered windows dropped beneath him. Four stories rose above him. The shuttered windows were like closed eyes. They refused to see him.

He might manage to climb down along the shutters, but before he had descended a single story the men from the hall would have the door down and would shoot him off the side of the building. He could see his own body lying small and sprawling in the inner court below, dim in the shadow into which the rain was dropping, dropping out of sight.

He turned, drawing the automatic. The door was shuddering. It bowed in with a groan under the weight of several shoulders that struck it in the same instant.

"Stop that. Stand back, all of you," said the Doctor.

"Lemme get through at him," answered a panting man. "He'll be out the window in another minute."

"He won't try the window," said the Doctor, with assurance.

A hand tapped on the door.

"Well, Witherby?" called the Doctor.

"How are you, Doctor?" asked John Witherby.

"Just a little sleepy. It's a shade early in the morning for me, old fellow," said the Doctor, affectionately.

Witherby laughed. His fingers were moving. They wanted to have the throat of the Doctor inside their grasp. But Witherby was laughing, honestly.

"I'm glad the boys haven't hurt you," said the Doctor.

"Ay. You'd rather do that yourself," said Witherby.

"Not at all, John. Not at all! You don't fathom me or my intentions. Just open that door and let me make you a proposition. You see that I want you, shamelessly. I want you at a high price."

Witherby frowned. He was, at this moment, half a stride from death. And if he entered the service of the Doctor that service itself might lead to death before long. But life itself would remain for Witherby, the sweetness of life, during whatever interval came between. It seemed that the taste of existence was in his blood—or was that the whisky?

"Well?" called the Doctor.

"Wait a minute," said Witherby.

He filled another glass and was about to drink, when a sudden loathing made him throw the glass out the window. The liquid splashed out of it into the air. The whisky had a bright red gleam against the gray. It dropped from sight.

Far below, he heard the light crunch of the glass against the pavement.

"Doctor," said Witherby, "I'll see you damned before I work for you."

"Do you mean it? You mean it Well, God have mercy on you, John. I'm giving the devil a prize when I send you to him. He'll have to catch you in both hands, however. Now, boys, have that door down and go in and get him."

There was a rapid trampling of feet. The door grunted like a hurt, living thing. It sagged, but snapped back into shape after the blow.

"Once more, all together, and we'll have it down!" called the Doctor.

WITHERBY LIFTED AT the top of the table. It came off. Merely its weight, as he had guessed, attached it to its standard, which was a heavy frame with a square top.

A second charge rumbled down the hall. The blow boomed with a crunching sound in it—the door had cracked from top to bottom.

Witherby slipped the automatic into his pocket and swung the weight of the frame shoulder high.

"Now—now—now!" he heard the Doctor urging.

The charge came again. It split open the panels of the broken door. Men with contorted faces, men with guns, burst in at Witherby. He hurled the frame at them. They went down like pins. He had a glimpse of one hand that pointed a gun at the ceiling in falling, and fired a stream of bullets into the plaster.

It was only a glimpse that Witherby had. Then he was leaping into the darkness of the hall. Other forms were in there, but all that he could make out was the long, pale face of the Doctor. For Witherby, it seemed to shine with a phosphorescent light.

He struck at that face. There was not time to get out his automatic. His fist failed to strike home. It was the lunging weight of his shoulder that knocked the Doctor flat. The same shock pitched Witherby off balance, and he dived under the streaming fire from two guns against the legs of the marksmen. They dropped on him.

Their guns had found a target somewhere. A man was screaming horribly, back there. But Witherby came to his feet with the automatic in his grasp, held by the barrel. A fellow came at him with empty hands, his arms flung out for a tackle. Witherby beat in the face with the butt of his gun and ran on.

The door at the end of the hall was ajar. A bullet from behind him knocked the door open, and Witherby darted through. He was down the steps, through the passage below, and suddenly he was standing in the big dance hall.

It was empty. One or two lights burned. That was all. They did not reveal the big chamber. They simply looked at it. The air was horribly stale with old cigarette smoke and the rankness of cigars. One or two chairs were overturned; some of the table cloths dripped to the floor.

He had only a glimpse of this unclean, silent place. His own speed seemed to bring the room to life as he crossed it.

One window was partially up. He jerked it wide, slid through, stood with the rain blowing gently against his face. There by the curb stood a taxi, the driver slumped over the wheel, asleep. Witherby grasped him by the shoulder, then stepped into the car. The driver gave him a gloomy look, suddenly became awake. Out of Kelcy's came thin voices, the rumbling of running feet.

A window opened above the taxi as it started. The thin voices clove through the dimness of the dream and entered the reality of day.

"Stop that damned taxi! Stop it, you—"

A bullet clipped through the top of the cab, drove a hole through the shatterproof glass of a window. But the driver merely hunched lower and shot his car around the corner in second.

He changed up and they whirred down the street.

Witherby could hear long, pulsing screams, he thought. But then he realized that the shrieking was in his brain.

Something was receding from him. It was the force of the whisky. It had eaten away half of his strength like a vile leech; it had sucked the blood and the heart out of him.

No, it was the girl who had killed in him something more vital than the strength of his body. The last of faith was gone, and she had killed it.

Somewhere she was stretched in bed, smiling in her sleep, confident that she had earned the praise of the Doctor. Witherby wanted to curse her, but the words died in his throat.

HE LEFT THE cab after riding a dozen blocks. He gave the fellow a hundred dollars to stop the bullet holes.

The man looked at the money, at the broken glass, shrugged his shoulders. He grinned at Witherby. He was a rat, but he was a game rat.

"You ask Kelcy for another hundred," said Witherby.

"Yeah, sure," said the driver, and eased his car off down the street.

Witherby went back to the hotel. The room clerk lay back his chair behind the reception desk. His head lay on one shoulder. His mouth was open. If his throat had been cut the picture would have been perfect. But Witherby went up the stairs instead of using the elevator. It was a lucky chance that no one would be able to fix the hour of his return.

In his small room he took another sponge bath, jerked off his clothes, slid into the bed. He set his mind for three hours hence. Then he went instantly to sleep.

He breathed very deeply. Now and then a greater breath than others heaved his breast. The light of day, increasing, flowed over his face without disturbing him. There were great troubles in his mind, however. For he saw in his dreams Cherry Larue, as dishevelled and unkempt and ruined as the great dance hall at Kelcy's, seen by the light of the dawn.

7

"DEATH BEHIND US STANDS"

AT THE END of three hours, precisely, the subconscious mind of the sleeper touched the conscious. He wakened, threw one puzzled glance about him, and instantly was out of the bed and preparing for this day.

The night before had been the longest in his life. While he was washing and shaving he went over the details. There was still a faint cloud in his mind from the whisky he had drunk, but this cloud rapidly dissipated. By the time he had finished setting-up exercises he was as fit as ever. There remained only one wound, and that was of the spirit. But he told himself that he would soon have the girl out of his mind.

Now and then a darkness crossed his thoughts. It was the reflection of his own stern, hard face in the mirror. For such a fellow as himself, what *was* happiness?

He wanted a drink of whisky. He wanted it badly.

He took hold of that appetite with a physical gesture and threw it away from him. He had two ways of meeting a temptation. One was to throw himself wildly along the course of the impulse. The other was to throttle desire and smile in its face as it died.

The old man had produced a sawed-off
shotgun from under the bed-covers

He killed that wish to drink, now. Then he left the hotel
to go hunting for the place of Granduncle Daniel Finley.

He wanted to walk. The place was only three miles from
the edge of town and three miles was nothing to him. He
found the Tilney Road easily. Half a mile of it put him over
a hill and out of sight of the town. When he looked back,
there was only a rising haze, a dimness cast up towards the
heavens. At night the city poured radiance into the dark
sky; in the day it radiated the fumes of darkness towards
the sun. It was unnatural. It was foul.

He was glad to face forward to the country.

The rain was over. Great white clouds rolled over the
edges of the hills, launched into the air, and floated heavily
overhead. They streaked bands of shadow across the coun-

tryside. But except for those strips of shadow the undried hills were burnished by wetness and the sun.

The ground was rolling. In parts of the world this rocky soil would have been given over to pasture, only; or else the bristling forest would have been allowed to turn all the acres green in summer and cover them with smoke in winter. But here industrious generations had been busy furrowing the soil, wearing it from the face of the rocks, lifting the rocks into piles, or working them into the heavy fences that went crookedly across the hills. The earth still was pushing her bones through her skin, a hard, unkindly earth. She was bidding the farmer defiance. She was trying to make this, once more, a paradise for the wild beast and the still wilder hunter.

Witherby, taking heed of that struggle, hoped that the ground would win. He was no lover of civilization.

He must have covered between one and two miles when he began to look about him. There was no sign of a house beside the road. Every now and then a lane turned off from the main highway and wandered quickly out of view among the trees, or ducked away over a rising bit of ground.

A rattling and groaning came up the road. It rounded the corner in the form of a tall old man. He was leading, not driving, a tall old horse which was hitched to a cart piled mountain-high with firewood.

"You know the Finley place?" asked Witherby.

The old farmer looked him in the eye with a sudden jerk of the head. He might be fifty-five; he might be seventy. It all depended upon what he had done in life and what life had done to him. The hot summers, here, and the winter frosts, fretted and worried even the faces of the rocks with premature age.

"Yeah. I know the Finley place," said the farmer, and stalked on by, beside his horse.

Witherby stared after the retreating group. He saw the great, shaggy hoofs and fetlocks of the horse rising and falling; the cart wallowed into a rut, threw off an unregarded stick of wood, and then swayed out of view around the next turn.

This old man knew the Finley place. He knew no good of it, also. That much was clear.

HE HAD HARDLY faced up the road again when a boy came by on the bare back of a pot-bellied old mare. Witherby stared again. He had a feeling that he had walked out of the machine age and into a remote past.

"You know where I can find the Daniel Finley place, son?" he asked.

The boy pulled on the reins and shouted: "Whoa!" He pushed back his hat and began to scratch his head. The hair stood up without waiting for the scratching.

"The which place?" asked the boy.

"The Daniel Finley place."

The boy stared helplessly around him.

"Maybe you can't find the Finley place—but the Finley place can sure find you," he said, and bumped his heels against the ribs of the mare.

She pulled in her chin, arched her neck with a foolish pride, and went thumping off down the road again. The boy turned and stared over his shoulder, his head bobbing up and down in a queer mockery as he looked back towards the stranger.

"A nice lot of people!" said Witherby.

He walked on around the bend. There was still no sight of a house near the road, though he could follow its windings, from this point, for another pair of miles. A big, brownfaced man came over the field with a dog before him and a shotgun in his hand. As he stepped into the road, Witherby walked up to him.

"Where's the Daniel Finley place?" asked Witherby.

The ox-like expression of dull-eyed content vanished instantly from the face of the big fellow.

"You want the place or the Daniel on it?" he asked.

He grinned impudently at his own remark and then started away. Witherby jumped after him and touched his shoulder.

"Well?" said the countryman, scowling, turning with an air of battle.

"You're the third man I've asked about the Finley place," said Witherby, "and I haven't had answer yet."

"Them that ask fool questions get fool answers," said the other.

Witherby laid his grip on the wrist of the farmer, who grunted and jerked back his other hand as though to strike. But he thought better of that. The fire that burned his arm to the bone was too much for him.

"Quit it," he gasped.

Witherby released him but remained standing close, too close for that shotgun to be used. The hunting dog came back and snarled, and sniffed at the legs of the stranger.

"What would you want to be knowing about the Finley place for, anyway?" asked the farmer.

"Why shouldn't I want to know about it?"

"It never gave anything but bad luck to other folks; not to anybody other than Finley."

"What has it given to him, then?"

The farmer was rubbing his wrist as he replied: "It gave him a hundred thousand a year for about fifty years, and I guess that's something!"

A hundred thousand a year for fifty years. That is five million dollars.

"Where is the house?"

"You take the next lane on your right and walk half a mile. That'll bring you to the house, and old Daniel, I reckon." He measured the stranger with his eye and shook his head: "But if you're gonna get a job working for him— God help you!"

"So long," said Witherby, "and thanks."

"Wait a minute," called the farmer, behind him. "The next time you come out around here with your damned tricks in your fingers, you're gunna catch hell. You hear me telling you?"

Witherby went on without turning. The men out here was as hard as their native hills, as full of rock; but he was used to hard men and plenty of them. Lascars are hard men in their sneaking way; the Gurkhas are hard men, too, in their native country or out of it; a first mate with a marlin-spike is one of the hardest, or a Scotchman with a stomach full of anger.

Witherby walked to the lane, turned up it the half mile, and came over a hill into view of a long building with a scrap of garden around one end of it, which was the house, and a stack of manure outside the other end of it, which was the barn. From pigs and chickens to men, all under one roof.

WITHERBY FOUND THE kitchen door with the sure instinct of a tramp. A tall woman answered his knock. She wore a calico dress and a long gingham apron, the blue of it worn and faded by many washings. On her feet were the oversize shoes of a man, turning sharply over at the heels. Witherby tipped his hat.

"This the Daniel Finley house?" he asked.

The woman regarded him with a stony face. There was no expression in her except malice. That was the only passion which she had known for years. The mask had been painted in an evil moment, but it had been worn until it had become a deathless part of the flesh.

"What might you be wanting?" she asked.

"Daniel Finley."

"You can't have him," she said, and shut the door in his face.

Witherby stepped back. He looked about him in such a quandary, and with such anger in his breast, that he decided to sit down on a big bowlder that stood near the house. As he sat there, he began to listen to the cackling of the chickens which were spreading everywhere. Some of their white or speckled feathers had been trampled into the ground, buried, stained, corrupted with earth.

A hundred thousand a year, for fifty years!

He looked over the old lines of the building, house and barn. He could believe that no good had ever come out of the place, except to Daniel Finley.

His hand touched a smooth place on the stone. He looked down and saw that a flat had been chiseled into the jaggedness of the rock and on the smooth surface was carved: "Stout Joseph Finley carried this stone three paces, October 7, 1743."

Underneath was engraved in small letters the cheerful couplet:

> "Vain is the might of hands;
> Death behind us stands."

He stood up, frowning. He leaned, got a good grip on two projecting knobs, and lifted. He kept on lifting until his shoes began to drive into the moist earth and there was an ominous crackling of threads in the seams of his clothes.

Then he straightened and regarded the bowlder with astonishment. He had not budged the mass. He had never met in all his journeys a man who could compare with him in strength, and yet there lay the writing on the stone: "Stout Joseph Finley carried this stone three paces, October 7, 1743."

He was breathing hard. He stepped away. His feet came out of the sockets that had been made for them in the soil with loud, sucking noises.

Well, inside that house might be Daniel Finley and he must be reached in spite of the termagants that might stand in the way.

He tapped on the door again.

"Whatcha want?" asked the snarling voice of the woman, inside.

He pushed the door open and stepped inside.

She was working at a kitchen table, carving cold meat with a long knife which had been ground so many times that it was almost eaten through, half way down the blade. She took this knife in a firmer grasp as she turned to Witherby.

"Get out, and get fast," she commanded.

He stared at her in a daze. He was still breathing hard from the great effort which he had just made. The blood was in his brain from the labor of his muscles. Out of the distance, he heard the sound of the voices of men in another room of the house.

"I'm John Witherby," he said. "My granduncle sent for me."

"You're John which?" she asked.

"John Witherby."

"You lie," said the woman. "John Witherby is in there right now, swappin' lies with Daniel Finley."

8

THE SPAT OF THE BULLET

THE DOCTOR, THOUGHT Witherby, probably had a hand in this, somewhere.

"I'll go in and find out about the other fellow who's carrying my name," said Witherby.

"You'll get out," said the other.

There was a bright, gray devil in her eyes. She walked straight towards him. And suddenly Witherby turned and stepped from the room to the outside. Small, icy shudders were chasing up his spine.

He could still hear the murmur of the voices of men. One of them laughed. It was a young, rich, confident laughter. That must be coming out of the throat of the other John Witherby.

Witherby went around to the front of the house. The door was locked. He turned the knob, braced himself, increased the pressure. Something groaned; there was a rapid tremor; the door opened almost soundlessly and let Witherby into a narrow hall. The wide floor-boards had been worn by the feet of many generations. The wall paper was so faded that the pattern had almost disappeared in many places.

What was more important was that the noise of voices

was nearer. He opened the first door on his left and looked into the shadowy eyes of a death's-head, a very old man with a great skull and the neck of a mummy to support it. He was all brown and wrinkles. Age without sun will turn the skin brown. Witherby remembered. Age will also draw on the cheeks until the lips seem to smile. And the lips of this ancient fellow were smiling without any real mirth.

At the foot of his bed, seated with crossed, jaunty legs, was a big young man.

"Get out!" said the death's-head.

Witherby walked in and closed the door. The big young man stood up.

"What in hell—?" he began.

Then he sprang back and reached a hand behind him. Witherby went after him with a bound. He wanted to hit for the jaw, but jaw-bones shattered like glass when he hit them with his balled fist. Shattering this jaw would keep the fellow from talking, and there were certain things that Witherby wanted to hear from this man. So he struck, instead, well up on the ribs, above the heart. The sound was like that of a drum beaten through a thick, muffling cloth.

And the big young man drove his shoulders back against the wall, sat down, fell over on his side. He had a gun in his hand, a huge, workmanlike automatic. This fell out of his fingers. He hugged his body with his hands. He writhed, kicking his legs slowly up and down. He could not swallow any air. Vainly he bit at it, twisting his contorted head over one shoulder.

Witherby stood back, after he had gathered up the automatic.

He saw that the old man had produced a sawed-off

shotgun from under the bed-covers. He was aiming this weapon at Witherby with a smile which was a great deal more than the faint grin of age.

"You hit him a good whang," he said, nodding. When he nodded it seemed as though the great head would snap off the wrinkled, lean neck that supported it. "But put down that gun, or I'm gunna turn you into a colander, all full of holes. There is iron junk and things in this gun, son."

Witherby put the gun back in his pocket.

"What you do it for?" asked the old man, not in excitement, not in anger, only in a rather pleased curiosity.

"Because he's a liar. You're Daniel Finley, I guess?"

"That's me."

"I'm your nephew, John Witherby. This liar was taking my name."

"You're my grand nephew, are you?" asked Finley. "Well, that was a grand punch you hit him. Bust any of his ribs, you think?"

"No. I think not."

The false John Witherby rose to his feet. Each breath he drew was a groan.

"If you're any blood of mine," said the old man, "you'll pay him back for that rib-roaster that he give you."

"I'll cut his heart out, for that!" grunted the other.

His face was more composed, now. He still had to breathe with his mouth wide open, but Witherby had a better view of handsome features, an excellent forehead. A beautiful face compared with the lean, stern face of the real John Witherby.

"Who are you?" asked Witherby.

"John Witherby, and I'm going to—"

"Did the Doctor send you here?"

The man's head jerked. The blow had clipped him like an unseen fist.

"Did you see that?" asked Witherby of Finley.

"I seen it," said the old man. "Who's the Doctor?"

"He's a crook in town. Anything up to murder. He tried to murder me last night—a couple of times."

"I don't see no scratches on you," said Daniel Finley.

"I'm not easy to scratch. You—what's your real name?"

"My name's John Witherby, and—"

"May I work on this punk?" asked Witherby.

"I seen the lie in his eyes, a minute ago," said Daniel Finley. "What you want to do to him?"

"Make him talk."

"I'll talk to a lawyer!" shouted the impostor. "I'll get the law."

"Go as far as you like with him," said Daniel Finley.

WITHERBY RAN HIS tongue over his lips, and smiled. The false Witherby, with a sudden groan of fear, reached behind him and caught from the floor a three-legged stool. Brandished by two of the legs, it made a formidable bludgeon, but Witherby picked it out of the air in full sway. He plucked it from the hands that grasped it. He took the false Witherby by the lapels of the coat and shook him.

The liar stopped struggling. His head wobbled crazily. Witherby let him stand still.

"Who are you?" he asked.

"Tom Carney."

"You lie. Carney's an Irish name. No Irishman was ever such a dirty crook as you are."

"I'm really Lester Partridge, but I work under the name of Carney."

"What's your work?"

"I'm a traveling salesman."

Witherby slapped the handsome face with the flat of his hand. The blow whitened the cheek of Partridge. It caused blood to run from his split lips.

"What's your work?" asked Witherby.

"No—no regular work," Partridge stammered.

"How long with the Doctor?"

"I never heard of him."

Witherby slapped the face again, with his palm and with the hard cracking knuckles of the back of his hand.

"How long with the Doctor?" asked Witherby.

Partridge stood with his eyes closed, his bloody mouth open.

"I never heard of the Doctor," he groaned. "My God, I never heard of him!"

"Make him talk!" chirped Daniel.

Instead, Witherby walked his prisoner to the open window and then pitched him through it head first. He landed, heavily, flat on his face. By degrees he picked himself up. Staggering, he walked away.

"Why didn't you make him talk?" demanded Daniel Finley.

"He made me sick," said Witherby, looking through the window. "He made me sick at the stomach."

"Maybe I'm gunna make you sicker," said Finley.

"How?"

"With this gun. Set down there where I can see all of you."

Witherby sat down.

"You're a man with a pair of hands," said Finley. "You're a man with a face to cover up a lie, too. You say your name is John Witherby?"

"Yes."

"What was your ma's maiden name?"

"Charlotte Finley."

"What kind of a looking woman?"

"She was tall and a little thin in the face, like most of the Finleys."

"She was a scrawny wench," said the old man. "But you might of seen pictures of her, that's all. The other one could talk about her, too. What sort was your father?"

"Happy-go-lucky."

"There was a lot of go in him, but there was damned little luck. What became of him?"

"He disappeared."

"When?"

"Eleven years ago. I was thirteen."

"Ever seen him since?"

"No."

"How old would he be now?"

"Forty-seven, about."

"Ever tried to find him?"

"Yes. For about seven years."

"Where had you looked?"

"All the way from hell to high-water."

Daniel Finley suddenly relaxed.

"Go on and talk," he said. "You sort of do me good. Where were you when my letter got to you?"

"Singapore."

"Doing what?"

"Drinking gin in a dive."

Daniel Finley began to laugh.

"You're John Witherby, all right," he said. "What was in the letter?"

"Come home to Daniel Finley three miles out on the road from the town of—"

"All right," broke in Finley. "If you ain't John Witherby, you're big enough to fill his shoes. That's all I care about. Come over here and—"

He had stretched out his scrawny hand towards his nephew. John Witherby was halfway to his feet. Then the bullet struck with an audible spat that slapped the head of the old man back against the pillow. Blood began to ooze from a little hole in the breast of the nightgown. The bullet had struck and the head had fallen back before Witherby heard the sound of the explosion in the distance.

9

THE UNFINISHED MESSAGE

WITHERBY LEAPED TO the window. The land ran away in a gradual slope, covered with brush, trees, big rocks. A hundred men could have hidden in positions which would have enabled them to look through the window at the man in the bed.

He would have leaped out of the window, gun in hand, but the faint voice of Daniel Finley called him back.

"Leave them be—leave them—come here."

He turned from the window and saw the tall form of the woman from the kitchen in the doorway. She had the same long butcher knife in her hand.

"You in here?" she snarled.

"Lizzie, shut up. It's my nephew—John Witherby," muttered Daniel Finley. "Here—John—"

Witherby was instantly beside the bed.

"Lizzie, get out!" breathed Finley.

Blood-bubbles burst on his lips.

"You're gunna die," said Lizzie, calmly. "You been shot through the lungs, and all the doctors can't save you."

"Take her out!" said Finley, more with movement of his lips than with vocal sounds.

Witherby turned on the hag.

"Touch me, and I'll ram this knife into your face!" said Lizzie.

And Witherby did not touch her. She turned, slowly, and strode like a man through the door, slamming it behind her.

Witherby flung one anxious glance towards the window through which the rifle bullet had come. It had to be a rifle bullet. The sound of the explosion had in it that metallic clang which distinguishes a rifle shot from that of a revolver. The man must have fired from a considerable distance. There had been an appreciable interval—say a third of a second, between the noise of the bullet striking the old man and the following sound of the explosion. Perhaps the marksman had been a couple of hundred yards away. A very small distance with the sun shining through the window on the target and the target itself the breadth of a man's breast.

These computations flashed in the mind of Witherby and went out in an unpleasant darkness of trouble as he saw that Lizzie had been perfectly right.

Death was hardly a step from Daniel Finley. The little blood-bubbles were forming and breaking on his lips again as he held out towards Witherby a small tin—a bit of roundness to be held between thumb and forefinger. It was, in fact, a cheap little yard measure made to wind back on a spring into the tin container. It was the sort of thing that could be dropped into a vest pocket.

This was what the old man held out to his nephew in a significant way.

"Two million dollars—nigh to two million dollars!" he whispered.

He paused in his talk. Even those few words had cost

him such an effort that his eyes were thrusting out to fill the shadowy hollows beneath his brows.

Did he mean that there were two million dollars in that ruler?

"Don't talk—hold your breath—I'll have a doctor here—"

"Fool—listen!" said Daniel Finley.

He made a gesture with both hands. Big John Witherby obediently opened the tape measure. There was meaning on the face of it, a number of little characters and figures in ink, scratched above or under the big print in which the inches were inked.

The old man, staring at it, took his hand from his wounded breast and caught the edge of the tape between thumb and forefinger.

He started to speak. The result was a horrible gasping, choking, bubbling sound.

And in a convulsion, fighting for breath and life, old Daniel Finley writhed off the bed and lay prone on the floor.

Witherby leaned to pick him up. Then he saw that on the pale boards of the floor Finley was writing with a desperate forefinger which found plenty of red writing fluid at hand.

"Start from Powhassett—"

The hand stopped writing; old Daniel Finley buckled up in a contorted heap and moved no more. The cessation of the gasping could mean only one thing. Witherby made sure of it by turning Finley on his back. And it was true. Daniel Finley had died with the hiding place of his two million dollars still unknown.

Was it not that which he had meant?

"Start from Powhassett." And then, the mystery could be explained by an interpretation of the characters on the little yard measure.

But who under heaven would ever be able to make that interpretation?

HE LOOKED AT the measure. Where the dying man had gripped the edge of the tape between thumb and forefinger, he had left a slight blotch of red blood on the cloth, and immediately under the red spot appeared the big number 9 for the ninth inch. Above the nine there was inked in a cross.

The cross over nine had to do with a most intimate part of the mystery, of course.

He had the tape measure in his pocket. He gave half a second to lifting Daniel Finley onto the bed. Then he rushed through the kitchen, merely snapping over his shoulder at the angular back of Lizzie: "He's dead!"

Then he jerked the door open and ran up the hill to the side of the house.

A stone fence lifted. He jumped it in his full stride. He jumped the deep-banked run of water beyond the fence. Straight for the ridge of the hill he kept on sprinting, automatic in hand. But when he reached the crest he saw before him an endless thicket which wavered up and down with the lie of the land towards the horizon.

There would be no hunting of a fugitive through such terrain as this. He remained on the hilltop, groaning, gritting his teeth.

"Start from Powhassett!" he kept muttering to himself. The words were tucked back in his mind together with another phrase: "Cross over nine."

Two million dollars!

He turned back towards the house. His blood ran cold and thin when he thought of such a fortune. If there were a sum of money like that in the air, and such a practiced devil as the Doctor to know of it and ferret out its hiding place. It was indeed not strange that John Witherby had walked into a stream of bullets shortly after his arrival in the town.

How much did the Doctor know?

Certainly he did not know where the millions could be found, or he would have had his hands on the money long before the death of the owner of the treasure.

The murder of Daniel Finley was the greatest part of the mystery. Or did the doctor choose to kill the old man rather than to permit the treasure to fall into the hands of John Witherby?

It might be that. But the long, pale face of the Doctor was not that of a man who lives chiefly for malice. Power and plunder were his goals.

But perhaps the slaying of the old man was the act of one not directly inspired by the Doctor. It might be the hand of Partridge that had fired the bullet.

But two million dollars!

On a reasonable investment, that meant an income of a hundred thousand a year. That meant two thousand a week. That meant three hundred a day. Three hundred dollars a day!

He took in a quick breath. The whole beauty of the world, every great sight that he had ever seen, poured in one great vision across his brain, one vision seen through a mist of golden light.

The thought of the money disappeared. There was

blood on it. The blood of murdered Daniel Finley would be the treasure, even if it remained underground, until the murderer was brought to justice.

HE WENT BACK into the house, through the kitchen door.

On the stove, drawn to the back, a stew was simmering. The sharp scent of onions was in the air. The sweat of the cookery was on the window panes.

He walked through to the room of his granduncle and found Lizzie bent over the body. One of her feet was touching the words written in thin red across the floor.

"Start from Powhassett."

When she felt the presence of the man behind her, she slowly straightened.

"All the Finleys was hard," she said, without turning to Witherby. "And he was the hardest, and the meanest, and the poisonest of the lot. He was the worst man and the meanest man and the hardest man that I ever seen in my life!"

She turned towards Witherby, and he was stricken with amazement to see that tears were running down her face. Her features were set in lines that were still harder than stone. Her eyes gleamed emotionless and bright as ever. But the tears were there on her face. It was a thing to be seen, and even then to be disbelieved.

"Is there an automobile on the place?" he asked.

"Bah!" said Lizzie. "Automobile, my foot! There ain't anything but the gray mare. Ride her in to tell the coroner."

And she stalked past him into the hall, her heavy shoes making a loud noise all the way to the kitchen.

He looked for a moment into the face of the dead man. There was no smile on it. Neither was there a trace of the last convulsion. He lay with an expression of perfect peace on his face. Death made him seem younger.

It was not affection that stirred Witherby, but the strange awe and pride of blood rose in him. Whatever evil the old man had accomplished, it was murder that had brought him to his end.

And now that crime had to be penalized. To Witherby, it seemed that justice would be worth more than two million dollars.

He walked back into the kitchen.

"What's your last name?" he asked of Lizzie.

"Who but a Finley would of stayed in the house with that old devil?" she demanded.

"A cousin?" he asked.

"One of them that don't count."

"Tell me where Powhassett is," he asked.

"I'll tell you when you're ridin' on the back of the gray mare," she answered.

"Where shall I find her?"

"Out yonder in the pasture."

He walked out into the open. The wind had moved away the last of the clouds. There was a deep, soft sound of insects humming through the summer air. Peace seemed to have covered the earth with the death of Daniel Finley.

10

"START FROM POWHASSETT"

THE GRAY MARE was in the pasture. Looking at her from behind, seeing the strong, square quarters and the straight legs, let down low for speed, she seemed a good one to Witherby. Then she turned her head and he saw the front of her. She had a ewe-neck, a long head, and a downturning muzzle that gave her the look of a fool. Like a fool, too, she stood while he caught her by the mane, and then she came lurching after him with unwilling steps.

In the stable he found a saddle. She groaned sadly while he was pulling up the cinches. But when he had mounted her she promptly pitched him on his head.

He sat up. The world stopped spinning. The gray mare was cropping grass beside the fence, the bit rattling back and forth against her teeth. Behind the glass of the kitchen window, Witherby could see Lizzie Finley, agape with laughter, like an image under water. Heartily he wished the simile were the fact.

He tried the mare again. He had sat out the frantic pitching of many a mustang in the West but this long, low creature moved like a snake. Ninety seconds later she spun like a top and hurled him clear over the top of the fence.

He forgot the murder of Daniel Finley. He forgot two

million hidden dollars. Nothing existed for him except the face behind the kitchen window, and this gray devil. An hour later, blood was trickling from his nose. He felt that he had been beaten with a club across the base of the brain. But the gray mare hung her head, beaten.

He dismounted, went into the kitchen, and found Lizzie Finley filling a granite-ware basin with water from the tap. She warmed the water with a supply from the hot-water kettle, and gave it to him. Silently he washed the blood from his face. His hands were shaking a little. He had not received such a beating in years; not since a certain Scotch-Irishman had fought with him in the narrows of a pass in Tahiti.

Lizzie Finley tossed him a fresh roller-towel. He dried himself with it, slowly, while his head cleared.

"Now, then—about Powhassett?" he asked the woman.

"There is two Powhassetts. One is a mountain and one is a river," she said.

" 'Start from Powhassett,' " he quoted, gloomily.

"There's plenty of Powhassetts to start from," said Lizzie Finley, dryly.

"If a man can make the right start and go the right direction, you know what he'll come to?" he asked.

"To two million dollars," she answered.

She began to mix dough in a pan with her bare, bony hands. And Witherby stared at her helplessly. She was carrying on the affairs of life. To her, they seemed to be kitchen affairs, only.

And in the downstairs bedroom lay her former master, dead.

"Why do you carry on, Lizzie?" he asked her, suddenly.

"Well, Dan'l is dead," she answered. "But you'll be hanging around for a while, till the heart's gone out of you!"

He went out to the mare again, mounted, and jogged her down the road towards town. He pulled the little tape measure from his pocket, unrolled it, and began to stare at the symbols which were marked on it. Above or below the numbers were zigzags, arrows, double lines, sometimes circles. He stared until the blind pattern of the markings struck into his mind; and always his glance rested, first and last, on the cross over the nine, with the little smudge of Daniel Finley's blood above it.

Somewhere in an old fairy tale, a drop of blood is made to speak and tell a great secret—or how did the old story go?

He could not help feeling that the bloodstain on the tape would reveal the truth to him, one day. That and the phrase: "Start from Powhassett!"

One could not very well start from a river, but the top of a mountain was a different matter. The vagueness of the problem made it big; the bigness of it made the mind of Witherby swell to meet the difficulty.

HE HALF EXPECTED the gunmen of the Doctor to appear at the windows that overlooked the street up which he rode into the town. But he got safely to the coroner. Nothing happened worth comment, except that people on the sidewalk turned and laughed at the sight of the rider of that grotesque gray mare.

The coroner went off for the scene of action in a big automobile. Witherby went back still riding the mare. She had a stumbling walk, a shuffling trot. When she galloped it was with one rhythm in the fore quarters and another in the hind. The rear legs seemed to be trying to run around the front. To save distance he tried her across country. And suddenly he forgot all about her faults of gait and appearance.

Off of her long hind legs she jumped like a kangaroo. When he set her a course she held to it, only varying from the straight line now and again to pick the low spot of a fence, the easiest way to brush through a hedge, or a stretch of smooth in place of the rough. Moreover, she poured herself out in a gallop that never wearied. By the time he reached the farm, he was half in love with the gray grotesque.

THE CORONER WAS already at the house. So was Thomas Holbrook, who introduced himself as the lawyer of the dead man. In the presence of the coroner and Lizzie Finley, Holbrook read off the will. It was very short, very characteristic.

"To my grand-nephew, John Witherby, I give and bequeath all my possessions and my love—because I've never had to see his wretched face, and because he never came howling to me for help.

"If he pleases, he can give Lizzie Finley a thousand dollars. She served me a good many years and she put a good, sour seasoning of meanness in every dish she cooked for my table.

"If John Witherby ever trusts a dollar of his money to the keeping of a bank, my curse goes to him as well as my fortune."

THE POST-MORTEM WAS as cursory as the coroner's speech to the jury he had gathered.

"Here is a character celebrated for hardness, hated by his neighbors, without a friend in the world. He has a stroke.

He realizes that he cannot live very long and therefore he sends for his grand-nephew—the only blood relation he does not hate. As John Witherby sits at the side of the sick man's bed, a rifle bullet is fired through the window and mortally wounds Daniel Finley. Only a few minutes before, Witherby has thrown an impostor through that window. Suspicion falls on that man, who called himself Partridge. But suspicion will also fall on a hundred of the neighbors of the dead man. He had offended scores of them mortally. Not a soul in the countryside had a good word to say for him.

"This is a case of clear murder by person or persons unknown; we must recommend the immediate apprehension of the above Partridge."

The coroner's jury did as it was directed; that same afternoon Daniel Finley was buried. He had expressed in his will his desire "to be buried on the Old Farm where I made my start."

The Old Farm lay five miles up the road from the New Farm. The Old Farm once had supported a big house, but fire had reduced it to a mound of charcoal inside the low, ruined walls of the foundation. The cellar steps were still clear. So in the lowest cellar room Witherby had the grave dug; there, in clammy darkness, the body of Daniel Finley was put to rest.

A crowd had assembled for the funeral, the sort of a crowd that comes to see the end of a great enemy. There were no wet eyes; there were no trembling lips. The mutterings that Witherby heard were deep in the throat, obscured by set teeth as often as not. Silently, for the most part, they watched.

Only Lizzie Finley made a slight exception. She was dressed up in her best gown, which was of a fashion at least twenty-five years out of the mode. Her coat had big shoulders; she wore a high collar with a lace edging; her hair was done high on her head and on top of the grizzled pompadour was set a tailored straw hat with a feather sticking briskly up at one side of the crown. She stood with folded arms during most of the little ceremony. After the damp earth had been packed in over the grave, she stuck a stiff little bouquet of flowers into the mound.

Then she climbed up to the surface with Witherby.

"Are you going to say anything to these people?" she asked Witherby.

"The minister has read the burial service," said Witherby. "I haven't anything to add to it."

"Well, I'll add something," she replied. "Listen to me, the lot of you."

They had been staring with bright, angry eyes at Witherby, as though they were transferring to the new owner a good portion of the hate they had borne towards the dead man. Now they looked at the queer face of Lizzie Finley, instead.

"You been hating him and ratting him all your lives," she told them. "You and your fathers, and some of your grandfathers before you. But he was too much for the lot of you. When he was a young man, he beat you with his fists. When he was an old man, he beat you with his brains. There's not a one of you that he didn't get the best of, one time or other. You know it. That's why you hate him. You're a pack of sulky dogs. If you hear a wolf growl, you run for cover. I wish there was another wolf, but all that's left is this poor half-breed. This here thing!"

She pointed with her thumb at Witherby, a gesture of high disdain. Then she strode away.

WITHERBY DID NOT wait for the crowd to disperse. He headed for a flat-topped eminence that had been pointed out to him as Powhassett Mountain. In a few minutes he had scaled it. It was a hill, not a mountain. It was not even a very high hill. But on the flat head of it there was a round of big stones as though it might have been an Indian fort in the old days. Witherby rolled some of those heavy stones out of the sockets into which they had settled in the course of centuries. Hungrily he moved them as though he expected to find beneath one of them that metal door which, in all Oriental tales, seals the entrance to the treasure chamber.

He checked this folly and began to look about him. Now that he was on the top of Powhassett, he could look down on the site of the Old Farm. The charred ruins of the house were small with distance. Powhassett River had its small beginnings on the southern breast of the hill and went sparkling through its little valley towards the east. Other hills, as tall or taller, rose up to block the rest of the view. Great trees had grown here. Great men with great hearts had harvested them. Now there remained the descendants, smaller, harder, wasting their lives on a wasted soil.

"Start from Powhassett." But in what direction? How far?

He unfurled the little tape measure again. The answer must be there in the writing. He would find the key. The cross over the nine was the heart of the mystery. Time and hard brainwork would enable him to decipher the puzzle.

11

CHERRY BRINGS A WARNING

WHEN HE CAME to the evening of that day, he was back in the house of dead Daniel Finley. It was the house of another man, now. That man was John Witherby. A rich man, John Witherby. A man, it appeared, who possessed fifty thousand dollars in cash in a bank, and certain thousands of acres of land—woodland, farming land. Rich John Witherby could either hold this ground or else he could sell it. He could hold it and try to lead a happy life among these sweeping hills, in this hateful community; or else he could sell and become a wealthy wanderer among the delights of the world.

There was no doubt in the mind of John Witherby as to what he would do until he came close to the house in the dusk and saw, behind the kitchen door, the looming outline of the great boulder which stout Joseph Finley had lifted and carried three paces, long ago.

He, John Witherby, had that same Finley blood flowing in him. If there had been a Hercules in the family those many generations ago, undoubtedly it was the same strain reappearing in him that made John Witherby so powerful.

He stood by the big rock and bumped his foot thoughtfully against it.

"Aye," said the hard voice of Lizzie Finley from the kitchen window, "there was men in this house, in those old days."

He walked into the kitchen and was pleasantly surprised to find that a dinner was in course of preparation.

"Look here, Lizzie," he said, "do you intend to stay on at this place?"

She turned her lean face towards him from the stove.

"Ain't I good enough for you?" she asked. "No, you'll want something young and pretty. She won't stay, I warrant you. Not for all your presents and not for all the silly love you'll give her. She won't stay and put up with this stove and the draughts in this house. And she'll cheat you in the market; she'll lie in her accounts. She'll be putting money in her pockets. She'll be laughin' behind your back. Aye, but I know what's in your mind. You don't want me. I ain't good enough for you. The mind of every young man is a foul mind!"

He looked through the savage malice in her face, tried to find an unhappy human soul and almost had a glimpse of it.

"Why do you want to stay?" he asked.

"Why do I want to stay? Do I want to go out and beg for a job? Do I want to go and show my ugly face at the doors of other houses and tell them that Lizzie Finley is beggin' for a job?"

"You don't have to beg for another job," said he. "You'll have plenty to live on. I'll give you a decent pension, Lizzie."

"Ha! That's it, is it?" she shouted. "I'm too old to work am I?"

"Ah, be still," said he, sighing, and walked into the front of the house.

Presently there was the clangor of the bell. He went into the dining room. Lizzie, with a black face, was putting down a bowl of fish chowder. Her claw-like hands were trembling.

"I'll be leavin' in the morning," she said.

"If you want to stay," said Witherby, "I'm glad to have you."

"You lie!" said the termagant. "It's a pretty face and a soft body that you want working for you here. Maybe you'll be marrying out of your kitchen, for all I know."

He looked up at her. Anger rushed through him. He shut it away from his face. He mastered it as he could master even the whisky thirst, when he chose. Calmly he said: "If you want to stay, I'm glad to have you."

She stared at him. Then she went back into the kitchen.

He drank the soup. It was thick and good. There was garlic in it. Where had she learned to put garlic in a soup like that?

She appeared, carried the soup plate away, served him with white slices of roast pork, apple sauce, sweet potatoes in a candy sauce, small brown fritters of fried parsnips.

"It's good," said he. He looked up and met her eyes. He surprised a deep question, a wonder in her look which disappeared at once.

"I ain't a fool," she said. "I ain't spent forty years at it for nothing."

"Tell me, Lizzie," he said. "Won't you be lonely here without Uncle Daniel to hate and damn?"

"You want to know?" she asked.

"Yes, I want to know why you want to stay."

"Because," she said, "I'm hungry to see who he pulls after him."

He stared at her.

"Who will Dan'l Finley pull after him?" she asked, almost dreamily. "He never give nothing but pain all his life. What'll he do now? He's died off the earth, but he ain't died out of this house. He's in the shadows and the corners of it still. And the ghost of him won't rest till he's pulled others into hell after him. Maybe me. Maybe you. Maybe the murderers! I want to wait and see."

It was from the heart. A ghoulish light was in her eyes, and the glimmer of it made him look suddenly down at his food. Evil was in her the shining light.

He pulled out a pencil and a bit of paper on which he made a series of those characters which were marked on the tape measure—the doubleheaded arrows and plain arrow, the wavy and the zigzag lines, the oddshaped hurdles, the circles with lines growing out of them, and that same cross which stood above the nine.

He pushed the paper towards Lizzie.

"Did you ever see my Uncle Daniel making signs like these?" he asked.

She peered at the figures. Then she shook her head.

"I never saw him," she confessed. "Why would he, anyway? What do they mean?"

"I wish I knew," said he, gloomily.

He crumpled the paper.

But crumpling it was not enough. Somewhere in those naked marks, divorced entirely from their places on the tape, might be the solution of the mystery. He had been a fool even to show the things to Lizzie Finley. Now, hastily, he lighted a match, set the paper aflame, and let it burn to an ash. When he looked up from this, he found Lizzie staring at him with a grim smile.

"Yeah," she said, "two million is a lot of money!"

She went into the kitchen, and he heard the snarling sound of her laughter, half stifled.

AFTER DINNER HE went into the front room. His bedroom would be on the second floor, because he had no wish to occupy the chamber where Daniel Finley had lain dead so recently. The parlor was of a type. It was carpeted with a design of big roses, and it was rubbed threadbare except in the corners. It might be a hundred years old. Certainly Daniel Finley himself would never have bought such an article. No, it must have been chosen by one of those women whose faded portraits looked patiently down at him, enduring time.

And their blood was in him, and the blood of those grim-faced men, all mustached or bearded.

Lizzie came to the door. He felt rather than heard her coming. It was perfectly soundless, but he found himself looking at the open door for an instant before her figure appeared. She seemed surprised by his waiting eyes.

"Anything else, John?" she asked him.

The use of his first name silenced him for an instant. Then he remembered that she was a Finley, after all.

"Nothing more," he said. "Good night."

After she was gone, he pulled out the tape measure once more. But the sight of it merely irritated him. The picture was almost perfectly in his mind. He could call up the mental picture and think of that with sufficient cohesion. But all the thinking led him to no end.

He put the tape down on the little center-table and began to pace the floor. Time slid away from him. His steps went up and down, endlessly. The moon was up. The window shade, hanging awry, allowed a slit of silver to appear against the lamp light.

Then he heard a quick pulsation of knocking at the front door. Fear must have been trailing him all the time. Now it leaped up in his throat and sent an electric prickling over his scalp. He grasped the butt of the automatic and set his teeth. The knocking came again.

The hall was unlighted. He was glad of the darkness as he walked into it. A man standing in a lighted entrance is the most perfect of all targets.

Then he heard his own hard, unreal voice saying:

"Who's there?"

"It's I! It's Cherry Larue!" called the voice of the girl.

The fear ran out of him. It thawed and disappeared and left a warmth of anger behind it.

He opened the door. She was wearing a cloak that made a mere bundle of her. There was nothing to be seen behind her on either side of the doorway.

"John," she said, "they're coming for you. They'll be here in a minute. You can't wait. Come quickly!"

"Step inside," said Witherby.

"There's no time! Believe me—"

He took her by the wrist and drew her in. He closed the door behind her, shutting her with him into the stale air of the house; but she brought with her a bit of freshness from the open night, and a little touch of fragrance.

"You don't understand what I mean!" she kept pleading, as he made her go before him down the hall. "The Doctor—and his best men—they're coming for you, John—"

He had her in the lighted room, at last. His memory had not done her justice. She was more than pretty. She was beautiful. Only, her beauty needed a little knowing. That was all.

"They were waiting for me the other night," he told her.

"I know they were. I didn't know it, then. All they told me was that you were to be kept out of the way for an hour or so."

"That was all, eh?" Witherby sneered.

"Ah, I see!" said the girl. She drew back from him a little. "You're not going to believe?"

"They brought you on purpose to that dive. On purpose to snag me?"

"Yes," she said.

"Who brought you? The Doctor?"

"Yes. No, it wasn't he. John Witherby, do you know that they'll be at this house in five minutes? Will you come?"

"Tell me the truth. They're out there now, and they sent you in to lead the poor ox outside. No reason why they should go to the trouble of breaking in, when they have you to lead a man out to the slaughter."

She caught a breath. Her eyes closed.

"You won't believe! I've got to make you, though. I've got to make you believe!"

"Anyway, it was a good party, the other night. I'm sorry it stopped before you told me your story. It would have been quite a yarn, eh?"

"John, for God's sake, believe me! They're coming for you. They'll murder you, certainly."

"And that'll make you cry, eh? About that story you were going to tell me, beautiful—that story of your life—how many men were in it?"

Not what he said but his way of saying it seemed to strike her white. She was silent for an instant.

"All right, then," she said. "I can't budge you—so I'll go back."

She was moving towards the door; he put out his arm and blocked the way. He drew his arm in, gathering her to him.

"You'll go back when I'm ready to have you go," said Witherby.

HER HEAD LAY on the crook of his arm. She looked straight up at him. One of her hands was against his breast but it exerted no pressure. She was not struggling. It was a miracle that no fear was in her eyes.

"Listen to me, you pretty rat," said Witherby. "You're the first one that ever got to me. I've seen a lot of your kind, but you're the first one that ever got to me. Maybe I'm getting old and simple-minded. Maybe I'm breaking up. And you got to me."

She only watched him, unanswering, with her eyes moving slowly across his face and up and down.

"By God, you know your business," said he. "I'll tell you how good you are. That other night—you almost made me love you."

"No, not almost," she said.

"You're that sure of yourself, eh?" said he. "You can afford to talk out, now—now that I realize your thugs are scattered all around the house? But before they have me dead inside it, some of them are going to hell. Know that? You were sure I loved you, were you?"

"Yes," she said.

And her eyes kept traveling over his face, calmly.

"How sure were you?" he asked.

"I could tell by a sort of panic in me. I've been close enough to the real thing before. I could recognize the panic, John."

"Oh, that's it, is it? You're telling me that I made *you* a little dizzy, eh?"

"It's true."

"My pretty mug—that's what turned your head, I suppose? Or was it my bright chatter?"

"I don't know what it was," she said. "Only, I knew—"

"What did you know?"

"I guessed, somehow, what you were. If I had dreamed that they meant murder—if I had dreamed that and I'd been on their side—don't you see that I would have warned them better against you? I would have told them to be ready for a tiger's charge."

"You're great at it," said he. "When I see how damned clever you are, I've a mind to pinch that gullet of yours, the way a woman pinches the throttle of a duck." He put the tip of his thumb and forefinger against her throat. In the soft of the flesh he could feel the heat and the throb of the great arteries. Her life was under his touch. At a gesture it would be gone.

"What a lot of hell I'd take out of the world—what a lot of hell for other men, if I rubbed you out!" said Witherby.

She shook her head.

"I won't do it, eh?"

She smiled at him, and shook her head again.

"Kiss me, John," she said.

A RESISTLESS POWER got hold of him and made his head bow. He resisted. Shudders ran through him as he fought against that impulse. But it bowed his head until he had kissed her lips. Once, and again, and again.

When he raised his head she looked up at him with sleepy eyes, like a child. She smiled again.

"And here you stand—and all the time the Doctor and his men are surrounding the house, eh?" he demanded, sneering—and trembling while he sneered.

She said nothing. As before, her eyes were drifting slowly over his face.

"They're closing in, eh?" said he.

"Yes," she said.

"And when they find you in here with me, they'll know you've been a traitor, won't they?"

"Yes."

"You're in danger of your life from them right now, Cherry?"

"Yes."

"What a liar you are—and what a blind fool you think I am!"

Again she made no answer, for a moment. Then she murmured: "It doesn't make much difference. You wouldn't have lasted long. You were made to die young."

"What do you mean by this sort of chatter? I don't follow it."

"I'll go with you," said the girl. "There was nothing but hell in front of me—and a dirty hell, at that."

"Cherry, what in hell are you talking about?"

"Love," she whispered. "Tell me you love me!"

"I love you, damn you," he said.

"I love you, John," said the girl.

"My God!" breathed Witherby. And: "My God, my God! It's true. You mean it."

"I do. All my heart means it."

"And what you say of the other night—that's true, too. You didn't know they were meaning to harm me?"

"Darling!" said Cherry Larue.

"Then you've told the truth now—and the Doctor and his devils are not yet around the house?"

"No—not yet—not quite—"

"Then, for God's sake let's start moving—"

"Shall we?" she asked, smiling up at him.

He took her by the shoulders and shook her a little.

"Come out of it, Cherry," he commanded.

She straightened, took a breath.

"All right," she said. "Quick, then—"

They were in the hall. "The woman upstairs—is she safe from them?" he asked.

"Safe as a statue," said the girl.

They went swiftly through the front door, he striding big, and Cherry running beside him to keep up, and close enough so that she touched him, continually.

"There's still another few minutes—ten minutes, John," she said.

And then, out of a bush on one side, from behind a rock on the other, he saw men rising.

12

HUNTED

THE MOON HAD been brightening the hillside, showing the gray mare grazing in the pasture like a ghost; but to the mind of Witherby danger flooded the countryside with an electric glare. It was the girl who had turned on the lights. If he died, she was the killer.

She stood still. She made no attempt to dodge away from him before the firing began. He noted that in the first tenth part of a second. Then he was diving towards a rock that jutted out of the ground.

Automatics began to chatter like machine guns. He hit the ground, rolled over and over, lay still behind his rock with his own gun in his grip.

"I got him! I got him!" yelled a voice.

"Cut in there between him and the house!" called the Doctor. "Good work, Cherry! Look sharp, everybody. You haven't got that terrier till he's dead."

It seemed to Witherby that he had been in the grasp of the Doctor all the time—every instant from the moment he stepped off the train into this trouble.

Twice the Doctor had closed his fingers and Witherby had managed to slip out of the grip; but this was the third time.

Out of the distance he heard the noise of the hoofs of horses. Riders were cutting in between him and the house—three men on horses.

He put a shot near the head of the leader. The trio scattered back into a dense growth of saplings near the house.

A hundred voices seemed to be yelling.

More guns roared. The top of the rock that sheltered him was crumbling. The whole rock shuddered with the weight of the lead that was plunging against it.

Without aiming, he reached around the side of the stone and sent a bullet uphill.

The firing from that quarter suddenly stopped.

Bullets began to throw dirt at him from the side. He saw in a shrub, like a figure seen through heavy rain, a marksman lying prone. Witherby put a slug in him, somewhere. The man screeched, leaped up, and fled.

The Doctor's voice was yelling: "Get away, Cherry! Stand out of line, you fool!"

Cherry was still there where she had first paused. She stood erect, the moon brilliant about her. It was as though she were frozen by the glory of the moment, the greatness of her victory over another sentimental sap of a man.

Witherby took her inside the sights. Instead of shooting, he spat on the ground.

Then, with a cloudy gesture, the moon was darkened. He did not wait for the cloud to pass completely over the face of the moon. Only the edges of the mist had exploded into white with the moon behind it when he got to his feet.

He wobbled from side to side as he made the sprinting start. He leaned far forward. He seemed to be falling face downward, but the driving power of his legs kept him making up the difference, precariously supporting him.

The bullets sang in the air about him. But not one touched his flesh. It was not so strange. The moon was lost, now, in the black heart of the cloud, and the sudden shadow was more baffling because of the clearness of the light the moment before.

Straight for the gray mare he went. She faced him, her ears back. Only at the last instant she wheeled away to gallop off. Before she had started, he was on her back, his left hand clutching her mane.

Was that the Doctor's voice which was raised into a siren sound of yelling dismay behind him?

Hoofs were beating. Not three riders but seven were racing towards him, three from the house, four out of a patch of trees up the hill. A light had come on in the top of the house. All of this had happened so quickly that, since the first shooting, Lizzie Finley had only had the time to jump from her bed and light a lamp.

And like something seen through the dimness of a storm, he made out the figure of Cherry Larue, still motionless in her unchanging place.

After that, the racing gallop of the gray mare jerked all thought of the others out of his head. She ran like a leaping devil.

He had to freshen the grip of knee and heel. Her thin mane stood up almost straight, quivering with the wind of her speed. Her head jerked back and forth. She seemed to be swimming through the air. The pulsation of the gallop went snapping through the brain of Witherby as he clung to the mare's writhing back.

A fence loomed, was gone behind him. She had leaped at the moon, now unsheathed from the cloud again. The great silver orb dazzled and shook before him. As the mare landed, Witherby slewed to the side.

A hair's weight of balance kept him from falling. He fought his way to an erect posture in time to steady himself for the next three jumps. The muscular sides of the mare kept his knees slipping up. The devil was in her.

She went straight at everything. She was not trying to get over the obstacles. She was simply trying to jump Witherby off her back, it seemed.

And with every jump she shook off the pursuit farther and farther.

If only she would keep to a straight line!

He looked back and saw little dark figures pop up against the sky and drop down again as seven riders cleared a stone fence. They were well back—far back—and then the gray mare headed into a ploughed field!

ONLY HALF OF it was ploughed but she seemed to prefer the soft going, though it soaked up her speed instantly. He pulled at her mane to swing her over. She merely veered more deeply into the ploughed ground, with her ugly head stuck straight out.

And the pursuit came up on the wind. Their shouts rang in the very ear of Witherby.

A crooked rail fence bounded the field. The mare came to it almost at a walk, buck-jumped it, and then lengthened her stride over the firm going beyond. They were shooting down a hillside towards the sheen of a lake. Thick copses rose here and there. Witherby saw the pointed roof of a little shack at his left—and the next instant he was in the air.

The mare had jumped big across a tiny rivulet and the unexpected leap shook the rider free.

The ground rose and slammed him. He saw the moon whirl around and around in the zenith.

"Charlie—Ad—cut around those woods to the right!" The Doctor's voice came out of the sky where the moon was wobbling to a halt after her merry-go-round. "Chan and Lew, go left, go left. The rest of you go straight through with me!"

Hoofs beat louder than the sound of exploding guns all around the prostrate body of Witherby. The pursuit went by. The horses seemed to be leaping like kangaroos. Getting to his knees, Witherby saw the riders pouring around the sides of a small wood, while the central trio hammered straight into the smoky darkness.

13

THE SHADOW OF THE SHACK

THE WIND WAS gone out of Witherby. He had to think fast, and his brain was numb. He had to move fast, and there was no strength in his limbs.

The Doctor and his men would discover, presently, that their quarry was not in the wood. They would find that the mare was galloping riderless in the distance. Then they would turn and take their backtrail to find the fugitive.

The little shack on his left looked like a refuge. It was probably unoccupied. It was hard to believe that lights had ever shone from the black face of it. So he ran stumbling to the door and pulled it open.

He had already stepped inside and drawn shut the door behind him when he realized, by the smell of cookery and the humid warmth of the inside air that he had been wrong—it was not an empty building.

At the same moment, he heard a slight metal sound of scratching. A great eye of light opened and caught him in the brilliance of its shaft. Behind it was a very dim figure that held a gun pointing towards him. The double mouth of the shotgun plainly entered the field of light.

"All right," said a husky voice. "Stand fast, burglar, and shove your hands up."

Witherby shoved up his hands.

About a shotgun, at close quarters, there is an inevitable logic. Argument is discouraged.

"I'm not a burglar," said Witherby.

"Ain't you?" asked the voice of the shadow. "Just taking a little stroll in the cool of the night, are you?"

"I've just squeezed out of the hands of a pack of thugs."

"Thugs, eh? Not men chasin' a horse-thief, or something?"

"No. Thugs."

"Keep your hands right up high. Keep trying to touch that rafter."

"I'm trying to."

"Try so hard that you keep on tiptoe. Now tell me who you are."

"I'm the nephew, the grandnephew, I mean to say—of Daniel Finley."

"Aha! You're the new Finley, are you?"

"My name's Witherby."

"It don't matter what your name is. It matters what your blood is. All the poison is in the Finley, I reckon. So you're the new Finley, are you?"

"Call me that, if you want. I'm up there in the Finley house, anyway."

"No, you ain't. You're down here in the Chet Wallace house."

"Glad to know you, Chet Wallace."

"How I wish to God," said Chet Wallace, "that I had all the rotten damn Finleys standin' there where you're standin'! How I wish that you was the last of 'em! Because I'd give you one barrel through the belly and one barrel through the head. If they took and hung me afterwards, I'd die laughin' to think that I'd rubbed out the Finleys, after all!"

"What have they done to you?"

"Nothin' but what's legal. For fifty years, old Dan'l Finley's been bleeding the heart out of everybody."

"How?"

"Lending fools money when they think they got to have it, and then turning around and taking their land and their houses and their horses and turning them out!"

There was a shadowy gesture behind the light. The barrels of the gun swerved a little.

"The Wallaces—we had as good a layout as folks would want. And then comes Dan'l Finley into the picture and we go smash. Twenty years he's eating on us. Twenty years we're paying him interest. We're working for him, starvin' for him, slavin' for him; and then he forecloses, and he's got our land, and we've got nothing. And—you're a Finley, are you?"

"My name's Witherby."

"You lie!" said the furious man. "You're a Finley."

"I'll tell you something, brother. I'm not ashamed of the Finley blood in me."

"Say that again!" shouted Chet Wallace.

"I'm not ashamed of the Finley blood in me."

"I'm more'n half-minded to let loose both barrels into you."

"One at a time," sneered Witherby. "One for the body and one for the head. Your first idea was the best one."

"You can be damn cool now and damn dead a minute later," said Chester Wallace.

"A lot of people have been that way," remarked Witherby.

"Keep them hands in the air!" commanded Wallace.

"My shoulders are getting tired," said Witherby, and kicked up swiftly without swaying his body—kicked as only dancing girls are supposed to. The toe of his shoe caught just under the muzzle of the gun and wrenched the weapon from the surprised hands of Wallace. The shotgun whirled into the air, clanged softly against a rafter, fell. Witherby caught it in his right hand. With the left the met the rush of Wallace. He put his hand against the chest of the big farmer and pushed. Chet Wallace staggered drunkenly back and whanged his shoulders against the wall.

WITHERBY FOLLOWED HIM. There was a bunk in the corner. He tossed the shotgun upon the blankets and took Wallace by the arm.

"Stand still," said Witherby.

"Leave go of me—you're breakin' the bones!" muttered Wallace.

"Let's be friendly," said Witherby.

"I'd rather be damned than have a Finley for a friend."

"Hush!" said Witherby. He could hear the beating of hoofs. He stretched his hand to the dark lantern, found the catch that moved the shutter, and slid it home across the eye of light. The round, white patch that embraced the door shrank to the thinnest of new moons, went out. The thick darkness filled the room like a black fog; the lack of light made it hard to breathe.

"Now what hellishness is in your Finley head?" asked Wallace.

"They're coming for me," said Witherby. "The thugs I was telling you about! Unless they go on by—"

But the Doctor would not go by. It was vain hope that, and in fact the hoofbeats moved straight up to the shack.

Witherby leaped, caught a rafter, swung himself up on it. He walked along the rafter to the wall. The rafter was not more than nine inches wide, but it would have to conceal him. He took off his coat, wadded it into the angle between the wall and the rafter, and then lay down on his side. Very little loose cloth would dangle about him, now; but of course the rafter was far too narrow to give him hiding. He would have to depend chiefly on one thing—that people see only what they expect and where they expect it.

A hand rapped at the door, which was instantly thrown open from the outside.

What would Wallace do? Half of everything depended upon that!

Exactly as before, he flashed the light of the dark lantern. It stopped the two men who were pressing through the doorway with a taller man behind him. The tall man was the Doctor.

Witherby, looking down, could see the pale face which seemed to shine with its own phosphorescent glow.

"Wait a minute, strangers," said Chet Wallace. "Wait a minute and maybe back up. What you want?"

"The rat that ducked in here," said one of the foremost. He was all red. His hair was red. His face was red. He had on a reddish leather coat, too. The devil was in the face of the Doctor, but the beast was in the face of this man. His upper lip kept pulling into a snarl; his nostrils expanded a little for each breath. "We want the man that came in here. Where is he?"

The breath of Witherby stopped. His whole chest became rigid with compressed air.

"There ain't nobody in here," said Wallace.

"No? We'll have a look at that," said the Doctor.

"If you fellows want two loads of buckshot in you—" began Wallace.

"You won't kill two men and get yourself smashed up by the rest of us," said the Doctor, quietly. "Don't let him bluff you, boys. Here—I'll go first."

They allowed him to wriggle through into the lead. The barrels of the shotgun were held steadily on him.

"I'm gunna blast you to hell—don't you move a foot!" Wallace exclaimed.

"Mind you," said the Doctor, "we're not going to harm you. We're not going to touch you or anything belonging to you. But—you'll have to let us search your house."

With that, he walked straight to Wallace and grasped the barrel of the shotgun in his hands, and shoved it to the side. The cold nerve of the act made Witherby bite his lip.

14

MAN HUNT

THE ACT OF the Doctor brought a grunt of satisfaction from the red-head. He came striding, his hands already reaching out, hungry to be employed, but the Doctor said: "Let him alone. Just watch him and let him alone. We want to search this place, not smash it. Don't touch anything. You hear me?"

Red groaned with disappointment. The Doctor was lighting a cigarette.

"Be ready, boys," he commanded. "If Witherby's in here, hell may begin to boil up around you at any moment. Where's there a lamp—and how do you come to be using a dark-lantern, my friend?"

"A man's got to look after himself when he's living alone," answered Wallace. "You ain't the first that have come here in the middle of the night. But the light and the looks of a gun were enough to keep the others out."

"Did you keep out Witherby, too?"

"Who's Witherby?"

"A biggish sort of a man. With a thin, hard, ugly sort of face; and shoulders that look sleek and fat—except that it isn't fat that they're sleeked over with. Did he come here?"

"I guess it was him that opened that door awhile back."

"Ha!" exclaimed the Doctor. "And he walked in on you?"

"He didn't knock. He just opened the door. I snapped on the light and had him. I told him I'd blow the gizzard out of him, and he didn't stop to talk. He turned and ran. He left the door open. I went and shut it."

"A couple of you get on your horses and ride back to the top of the hill," said the Doctor. "This man may be telling the truth. There's a light there—light that lamp, one of you."

It was lighted. It cast a dim beam over the unkempt room. Unwashed tin dishes were littered on the table. Some white streaks which looked like the drippings of batter were spotted down the face of the stove. Old clothes hung on nails along the walls.

And Witherby for the first time saw the face of Chet Wallace. The beard of three or four days was dark on his skin, leaving a surprising naked space around the eyes, that gave him the look of an ape. He was a tall man with powerful shoulders. The rest of his body lacked flesh. He was dressed in an undershirt and long drawers. The elbow of one shirt sleeve was in rags and showed the grimy skin. He had a sock on one foot. The other foot was naked. He was dressed as he had been garbed when he lay in the twist of his blankets, asleep. The noise of the passing horses and the voices must have roused him.

"Look everywhere," the Doctor was saying. "He's not here, I suppose. But look everywhere. He could press himself into one of the wrinkles of those blankets, if he wanted to. Leave that door open and get some decent air into this muggy den. That's right, Charlie."

"Charlie" was a very thin, dark fellow of forty who

"Look everywhere," the Doctor was saying. "He's not here"

opened the door and returned to his chief. He was apparently a lieutenant of importance. He did not join in the search but remained at the side of the Doctor.

"Cherry did a neat job of that," he said.

"She's always neat," said the Doctor, almost indifferently.

"Maybe Witherby's a half-wit, though," suggested Charlie.

"He's beaten me three times. Does that sound like a half-wit?" asked the Doctor through his teeth.

"Luck, only. Maybe it's only luck."

"Lightning doesn't strike three times in one place. Neither does luck," said the Doctor, tersely.

"If he's not a half-wit, why did he let her bring him out of the house? She'd sold him once before."

"There's always one girl to unlock the wits of every one man," said the Doctor. "She's the kind of poison that works on Witherby, that's all. If she's made a fool of him twice, she'll make a fool of him again."

"Would you try her on him again?"

"She'd be willing. She volunteered this trick tonight. I didn't expect it of her."

"You didn't?"

"No."

"You didn't have to build her for it?"

"Hell, no," said the Doctor. "She does this sort of thing for the fun she gets out of it. I don't have to pass over much money."

"The queer thing is," said Charlie, "she looks kind of straight and clean—just out of a bath."

"That's what does the work on Witherby, I suppose."

"Her eyes look kind of clean, I mean."

"If I don't get him this time, I'll send her straight back at him," said the Doctor.

"The devil you will! He'll wring her neck!"

"No. If she's made a fool of him twice, she'll be able to make a fool of him a thousand times. If I miss tonight, I'll send her straight back at him."

"Leave that box alone!" shouted Wallace, loudly.

A box nearly two feet square stood in a corner of the room. The redhead was opening it as Wallace shouted.

"Hey, what's the matter?" asked Red-head.

"Leave that alone or I'll knock your head off!" yelled Wallace.

"Open it up, Ad, and we'll have a look," said the Doctor.

Ad, lifting the lid, drew up from the inside of the box a pair of dolls: one, the image of a barefoot boy; one, a girl in

short skirts. Both of the dolls were badly soiled. The stuff-
ing protruded from the left leg of the boy.

"Damn you!" shouted Wallace, and made a lunge.

AD, DROPPING THE dolls, met the rush with a very nicely
timed straight right. It sat Wallace down with a thud. He
remained sitting, his hand clapped to his jaw. And picked
up the dolls again and laughed.

"Look at what he plays with!" cried Ad. "Look at what
the big baby goes and plays with when he's alone!"

"Put them back!" said the Doctor.

He went to the box and peered down into it.

Then, shaking his head, he replaced the dolls almost
reverently, and lowered the lid of the box.

He said to Wallace: "It's all right. We haven't touched
anything. I'm sorry about this."

"Why are you sorry?" asked Ad, gaping.

"Be still, you blundering fool," snapped the Doctor,
angrily.

And Ad was still. He merely chewed the air with his
open mouth for a moment, but no words came from him.

Witherby, understanding gradually what it was about,
felt the stinging of a sudden pity.

"What about upstairs?" asked the Doctor.

The Lamp was raised. Every part of the room had been
rummaged through by this time; as the lamp was raised,
all eyes swept upwards to search among the rafters towards
the ceiling.

On the eyes of Witherby the radiance fell with a shuddering as of waves. It was his own sudden trembling, he
knew.

He tried to look upwards himself. Glances attract

glances. Yet he could not keep his eyes away from the long, white, terrible face of the Doctor. When the shooting started, Witherby would try for one thing only—to kill the Doctor before he himself went to hell.

Were they not seeing him?

Chet Wallace, at least, was staring straight at him, with horror rounding the smallness of his eyes.

But no one else seemed to take note. The lamp lowered. The Doctor said: "He's gone through our fingers again. I don't blame anyone. I was right there on the ground with you, and he did me in along with the rest of you. Remember this: from now on, it'll be twice as hard to get at him. He'll be a little more scary than any hawk. Get out of here, all of you. You, stranger—I want to apologize for breaking in here like this. Here's twenty dollars for the trouble we've given you. And—one week from today you get another twenty if you haven't done any talking about this little visit."

Chet Wallace took the money and stared at it. He said nothing. The Doctor left. The noise of horses moved slowly away—snortings, singlings, the shock of hoofs on soft earth and the clash of them against rocks. This devil, the Doctor, knew perfectly well how to adapt his forces to the situation. His men in motor cars would have been useless to cross this semi-wilderness. But on horses, they could go anywhere.

Witherby dropped down from the rafter, his coat in his hand, and put it on. He breathed deeply, to fill the hollowness about his heart.

"Here's a hundred," he said to Chet Wallace. He put the

money out and added: "There'll be more than that. Come up to see me on the hill."

Wallace took the money with an absent hand. He continued to stare at the twenty which the Doctor had given.

"My God," said Wallace, "I'd have to save for two months to get this much hard cash!"

15

SINISTER ALLIES

THE DOCTOR AND his tribe might revisit the shack of Chet Wallace at any time during the night. They were almost certain to keep a watch over the Finley house against his possible return. Therefore Witherby went into the woods, broke off some evergreen branches, and lay down on a couch of these. More of them he placed over him.

A deadly chill passed out of them into his body. But he fixed his mind on other things. Presently he slept, and he did not waken until the dawn was pouring like cold fire through the trees.

The birds had begun. Their chattering stopped all around him as he stood up. He heard fluttering of wings, crackling of twigs overhead. Then the chorus was ringing him in from a distance. He was stiff, but a few movements made him warm enough again. He headed straight across the hills for the Finley place. If the Doctor's agents were watching, he would have daylight to use in spying out the spies.

His spirits rose a little as he walked, but still there was a hollowness around his heart. The treachery of the girl was at the base of that unhappy feeling. She must have entered him very deeply. The first treachery had not removed the thought of her entirely. Neither did this second betrayal enable him to forget her. He wondered if the Doctor were right—would he allow her to lead him a thousand times towards the slaughter?

On the way back, he passed three houses very like the Finley place itself. But these were empty—empty as his soul. Some of the lights had been knocked out of them and these windows had been boarded up.

He remembered what Wallace had told him. Perhaps these were all on the Finley estate. Once each house had supported a happy, numerous family; but Uncle Dan'l had devoured the property of each household and seized the land, and banished the old owners. Witherby could under-stand, in the light of this, why the crowd at the funeral had stood silently about, with hungry faces.

As he came towards the Finley house, he moved more slowly. But when the sun came up, slanting warmth and brightness into his face, he made up his mind that he could pay no more heed to the danger of the Doctor. He walked straight on, boldly.

In the pasture, he was surprised to see the ugly gray mare. She lifted her head and actually whinnied. She came towards him, and walked down the fence, reaching her head over it, making rattling, snuffing noises. He rubbed her muzzle with his fist. He patted her hard, crooked neck. When he came to the end of the fence he paused to wonder over her.

For some reason, she felt a devotion to him. And he was greatly moved. The bright, fierce little eyes had a red stain in them, still; but he knew that he would never again have any trouble controlling her.

He went on to the house and entered the kitchen door.

Lizzie was bending over the open fire box, prying at the wood inside with a crooked poker, a heavy bar of iron.

Her greeting was merely: "I'll thank God when a Finley will buy me a new poker."

"Give it to me," said Witherby.

He took the iron rod, wrapped a rag around the hot end of it, and exerted the full force of his hands. The iron yielded. It straightened, leaving only a small crook at the bending point.

"Here you are," said Witherby, and handed back the poker.

She took it with a look that had both fear and reverence in it. For a moment she stared down at the poker. Then she shrugged her skinny shoulders and turned back to her cookery.

"Been out drinkin' and foolin' around, have you?" she asked over her shoulder.

"It was a nice party," said Witherby.

He went into the front room, remembering the tape measure which he had left there. But it was gone.

The shock of that discovery turned every nerve to ice. But Lizzie, of course, had picked the thing up and put it away.

He went back to the kitchen, saying: "Where did you put the tape measure that was in the front room, Lizzie?"

"I didn't put it because I didn't see it," said Lizzie.

"You didn't see it?" exclaimed Witherby.

She turned suddenly on him.

"I'll show you something," said she.

She led the way back into the front room.

"Look!" she said, and pointed to a broken window-latch. "Somebody come in here last night. But would a tape measure be the kind of meat they wanted?"

She narrowed her eyes at him.

Had she stolen the thing herself and broken the window latch to offer her excuse?

She answered his thought. "It ain't money that I want. Not even two million dollars!"

And he was convinced, at least in part.

A MADDENING SENSE of helplessness baffled him. If they had stolen the tape it was because they knew that it was the key to the place where the treasure was hidden. That key was in the hands of people far keener than he. They would work out the problem. They would scoop in the money, which represented most of the savings of dead Daniel Finley. And Witherby would be left with the skimmed milk: he would have the farms and some fifty thousand dollars in the bank. An inheritance tax would slash away a great part of his holdings. He saw himself pinched out of a great fortune.

But that was not all. He had made up his mind, while he talked with Chet Wallace, that he would rectify some of the cruel injustices that had been worked on this community through the avarice of his granduncle. When he was through undoing some of the evil of the past, what would remain in his hands?

"Go wash your face and hands," Lizzie Finley was saying, "and set down at the table. I got popovers comin' up. You got three minutes to get to that table."

He got to the table in the three minutes. She brought him cracked wheat for cereal, and bacon and eggs with burning hot popovers. He ate hugely, and drank three cups of strong black coffee.

His spirits rose. The Doctor had beaten him, but the game might not be ended.

He said, as Lizzie poured his third cup: "Listen to me. You've been on the place for a long time. You know all about the affairs of my uncle."

"Nobody but the devil knows all about them," answered Lizzie Finley.

"You know the people he threw out of houses."

"I know 'em. They been cursing me with their eyes long enough. They'll be cursing you, too, and anything with Finley blood."

"Get on your Sunday clothes and go to every one of those people you can reach. Tell them to pack up and go back to their houses."

She folded her arms high on her chest.

"What good would the houses do? It ain't the houses that they've made a living out of," said Lizzie.

"Tell them that they get back the land, also."

"Ha!" grunted Lizzie. "You going to undo everything that your uncle managed?"

"I've got to."

"Afraid of these scum around here?"

"Last night, Lizzie," said Witherby, "while I was taking a little jaunt around the countryside—"

"I seen you starting off," said Lizzie, calmly, "and your playmates right after you."

"I wound up in the house of a man who hated the Finleys. His family had been dispossessed by Uncle Daniel, and he had a chance to lift a finger and turn me over to—those playmates of mine. But he didn't do it."

"He was a fool, then," said Lizzie Finley. "Don't you go and be a bigger fool than him."

He laughed at her, suddenly.

"You don't mean that, Lizzie," said he.

"D'you think that I don't? I'm a Finley, and a Finley gave me my hell on earth. Why should I cry about them that've been in hell along with me? No. I'd see 'em rot, first."

He pushed back his chair and rose.

"Will you go the rounds and tell those people?" he asked.

"They'll tell me I'm crazy."

"No. They'll save that word for me. Do what I've told you to do. I'm leaving for the day. I'll come back by night, I hope."

"Dead or alive?" asked the iron woman.

He shrugged his shoulders.

"I don't want to do too much guessing," he said.

"It ain't guessing that I'm doing," she told him. "It's knowing. Right now, I can see the skull under the flesh of your face. You're as dead as ever I seen."

He could not keep a mortal shudder out of his body.

"Do you often have second-sight?" he asked her.

"I smelled the dyin' of Uncle Dan'l for a month," she answered. "I used to sit up in the hall outside of his door, at night, and wait for the death-rattle." She turned and marched back into the kitchen.

WITHERBY WAS GLAD to get into the open. He saddled the gray mare and rode straight for the town. He could shorten the three miles, in this manner. And as he traveled, he saw a pair of automobiles, one behind the other, bucking

over the humps and hollows of the road that led from the
town towards the farm.

Were those emissaries of the Doctor, again? Had they
come for him or to begin the treasure-hunt?

A frantic impulse of nervousness made him tremble.
The eagerness of a bull-terrier for a battle was in his body
and his blood. But what could he find on which he might
set his teeth?

When he got into the town, he tethered the horse, got
a taxi, and went straight to the city hall.

The stale scent of cigar smoke adrift in the corridors of
polished stone was enough to tell him that he had entered
a political center. When he got to the office of the district
attorney he had to wait in the anteroom, outside a mahog-
any rail. He sat on a long bench with a dozen other people
who shoved to the left each time the end person on the
bench rose and went into the inner office.

He spent ten minutes in this manner. Then he said to the
beef-faced sergeant who was master of ceremonies: "I'm
the Witherby that inherits the Daniel Finley layout. Tell
that to your chief, will you?"

The sergeant pursed his lips till his moustache bristled
up against his nose. Then he pulled his mouth in and made
the moustache bristle in a downward direction.

"All right," he said. "I'll fix it, chief."

Two minutes later, Witherby sat at the side of the
great, shining desk. The district attorney was a man with
a pale, intellectual face. When he looked down, there was
a nervous fluttering of his left eyelid; that was his only
peculiarity.

He had shaken hands with great cordiality. He was very

glad to meet Mr. Witherby. He had seen Daniel Finley many times. What could he do for Daniel Finley's heir?

"Do you know the Doctor?" asked Witherby.

The glance of the district attorney went down to his desk again. The eyelids fluttered.

"The Doctor?" he said. "What Doctor?"

Witherby rose.

"That's all I wanted to know," he said.

"I don't understand," said the man of the law, rising in turn, looking baffled.

"I do, though," said Witherby.

"Doctor? Doctor? What doctor are you referring to?"

"The murdering crook who pays you such a fat lot of coin," said Witherby. "That's the one I mean."

"Young man—" said the district attorney.

"I wanted to tell you that he's after my hide," said Witherby. "I thought that the police might give me a hand. But I see how it is. So long."

"Wait a moment. In what you say there's an insinuation—"

But Witherby was out the door. He could have known that a fox of the caliber of the Doctor secured friends in high places. And the battle would have to be waged single-handed on the part of Witherby.

He went straight to the Ridgeview Hotel and up to his room. His approach to the door was soundless. He spent five minutes turning the key in the lock noiselessly. Then he thrust the door suddenly open.

He had been right. There was someone in the room but it was not a man. Against the brilliant square of the window he saw the silhouette of Cherry Larue.

16

BRISTLES OF DEATH

HE SHUT THE door quickly behind him and turned the catch that locked it. He noted two things—that she was rising from her chair and that she was not afraid.

He stepped past her, silently, and looked out the window. There was no one appearing in any of the opposite windows. Nothing dangled from the eaves above him; the pavement of the yard beneath was empty.

"The Doctor told you to drop in again, eh?" said Witherby, moving back from the window.

She shook her head.

"Sit down," he invited.

She lowered herself gradually to the arm of the chair. She had the considering eyes of one ready to flee from danger. And yet she was not afraid.

"Are you going to listen to me, John?" she asked.

"I love to listen to you," said Witherby.

"I'll tell you the straight of it. I went out to give you an honest warning. I didn't think that they would be out there so soon. According to the plans I heard, they were to arrive later. I thought I was getting you away into the clear."

He lighted a cigarette. The smoke had no taste. It was only a coolness in his deep lungs.

"How did you find my room?"

"The Doctor had you tracked."

"And he told you?"

"Yes."

"Sent you along to bring me out into the open?"

"He doesn't know that I'm here."

"How surprised he'd be!" said Witherby.

She said nothing. She kept watching.

He surveyed her again. All he had seen to this point was her face. It had focused his attention like a glaring headlight. Now he saw the soft brown tweed of her suit. She had on a silk blouse with a deep collar; and there was an orange tie that made a warm dash of color. There was orange, again, in her hat. Her shoes were heavy, broad-toed. They made her feet look ridiculously small.

"I like to look at you," said Witherby.

She said nothing, again.

"If they know where my room is, why don't they fix a plant—or are you the plant?"

"They've fixed a plant," she said.

"What sort, partner?"

She made a gesture towards the washbasin. His shaving things stood around the edge of it.

"Anthrax in your shaving brush," she said.

He went over and looked curiously at the brush.

"What's anthrax?" he said.

"It's a disease. They've filled that brush full of the germs. From sheep, I think. When you shave, the germs get into your blood through the little cuts on the skin."

"That's a nice idea."

"The Doctor has lots of nice ideas," she told him.

"How long have you been with him?"

"Six months."

"That's long enough to learn a good deal."

"I've learned a lot."

"You learned something to tell me when you came here today."

"Yes. I learned that, too."

"Fire away," said he.

"You may think that the Doctor will hold off, now that he's got what he wants."

"What did he want?"

"The tape measure. You know that."

"Did you steal the tape while you were in there with me?"

She drew a faint breath and looked at the floor.

"What have you got in that fist?" he asked.

"A handkerchief."

"Let me have it."

She passed it to him.

It was one of those small things. The linen was very sheer. It was wrinkled with pressure and slightly damp.

"You *are* a bit nervous," said he. He gave the handkerchief back to her.

"Yes, I'm a little nervous," she admitted. "I've got reason to be."

"What do you think I'll do?" he asked.

"Nothing," she said.

It made him so angry that he strode to her and leaned.

"Nothing, eh?" said Witherby.

"No. Nothing," she answered. And she bent back her head and looked straight up into his face.

"You have the nerve of a saint—or a hunting tiger," he told her. "I ought to break your neck for you."

She shook her head. That studious and progressive interest, as of a reader, was in her eyes again.

He took her under the armpits and lifted her to her feet. She was a limp weight. He lifted her still higher until her face was level with his own. Then she smiled at him a little.

"You're a strong boy, John," she said.

HE HELD HER there, easily.

"You're so full of the cold poison," he said, "that you'd kiss me now and think nothing of it."

"Not a thing," she answered.

"Do it, then," said Witherby.

She put a hand on each side of his face and kissed him between the eyes. He placed her on the floor again.

"It's true," said Witherby. "When I'm away from you I try to believe that I'll see the devil in your face the next time we meet. But I never do. I'm going crazy about you again."

She only smiled at him.

"Now let me have the rest of your talk," he commanded.

"I was telling you that the Doctor has the biggest thing he wants. He has the tape measure; when the riddle's taken off it, he's going to be rich. But that isn't all he wants. He wants you."

"What price?"

"He wants you dead."

"Does he? I'm not surprised."

"You've beaten him three times. No one else has ever done that. He's always been successful in everything. Now he's afraid that his men will begin to think that he's not infallible."

"He has another reason behind it."

"Yes. He hates you on his own account."

"That's a compliment. But why does he hate me?"

"Because he has a suspicion about me. He's not sure— but he thinks that I may like you quite a lot."

"Jealousy?"

"Yes."

"The Doctor loves you?"

"Yes."

"Must be a queer thing to see him in love."

"It is."

"I wonder if you'll tell me one stroke of truth. Do you belong to the Doctor?" He had to put it more brutally. "Are you his woman?"

He saw a pulse strike big in her throat. She grew pale.

"No," she said. "I don't belong to him."

"Who do you belong to?" he asked.

"To you," said the girl.

"By God," cried Witherby, softly, "when you lie to my face like this, it's hard for me to keep my hands off you. Do you think that I'm taken in by your damned lies?"

"I know you don't believe me," she said.

"Then why do you say such things?"

"Because they're true."

He turned away from her and leaned on the window sill again. He dragged down deep breaths.

"Now tell me—since the Doctor's after me—tell me what I'm to do."

"You're to leave the country."

"Ah? Run away, eh?"

"Yes."

"So he'll have a freer hand?"

She was silent. Then she said: "So that you won't be killed, John."

"If I run away, will you run with me?"

"Yes," she said.

"Will you go down the street and marry me this minute?"

"Yes," she said.

Something hummed higher than a buzzing wasp past his head. It struck solidly against the wall; the report of the rifle shot clanged loud and sharp immediately afterwards.

He jumped back from the window and looked past the girl. Her expression had not altered in the least. There was a hole in the wall; rains of plaster were running slowly down from it and making a tiny white heap on the floor.

17

UNDER THE GREAT STONE

"THAT WAS A close one," he said to the girl. "An inch more and I would have been draped over that window; and you would have collected the bonus. How much does the Doctor offer you if I'm bumped off?"

She stared at the small running of grains from the hole in the wall.

"And how did you manage to make the signal that told the marksman to be on the job?" he continued. "You're a clever girl, Cherry. The handiest that I ever ran into."

He began to pack his things, throwing them rapidly into the suitcase. Still she stood there like a stone. She had stood in that way the night before when the guns opened on him in the moonlight near the Finley house.

"Try me another time," said Witherby, as he finished his packing. "The Doctor says that even if you've been proved a crook a thousand times, I'll still play the fool about you. So come and try me another time."

She lowered herself into a chair. Her head bowed. She looked down at the floor and the brim of her hat shadowed her face so that he could not see the expression.

He picked up the suitcase and stood at the door, weighing it easily in the capacious grasp of one hand.

"The cards are a little bit stacked, in this game. You've got the police and the Doctor and the rest of his crew. I've got myself. But by God, I'm not a dead man, yet."

She did not move. Seen from this angle, as she remained bowed in the chair, she looked hardly larger than a child.

Downstairs, he paid his bill, gave the suitcase to a taxi driver, and paid him liberally in advance for taking the bag out to the Finley house.

Down the street, he bought a new shaving brush; at a five and ten cent store he bought one of the little round tin cases that held a thirty-six inch tape. It had exactly the same printing as that on which Daniel Finley had made the symbols.

The whole picture of them flashed clearly across his mind—so clearly that he was afraid that he might never see them better. He drew out his fountain pen; putting the tape on the edge of a counter, he wrote in the symbols from the first to the last. When he had finished, there was only one mark which remained unduplicated, and that was the small smudge of blood which had been like a pointer over the cross above the figure nine. But he could remember that blood-mark.

He went back to the gray mare and took her out of the town and across country to the Finley house. It was not a bad country, he thought.

HE WENT BY one of the houses which that very morning had remained blank of face. It was different, now. The boarding had been torn away from several of the broken windows. A Ford truck was backed up to the side door. And he could hear the strong voice of a man singing.

A pair of boys raced around the corner of the house.

They forgot their game of tag when they saw him. They began to yell, and point. They began to dance up and down, turning their heads, shouting over their shoulders.

A woman ran out of the side door. A man in overalls strode out to the porch. He began to wave his arm widely, in a greeting. The woman flourished both hands.

Witherby rammed a heel into the flank of the gray mare and sent her off at her long, reaching gallop.

But as she flew a fence he was thinking: "What am I around here? A damn good fairy, or something like that?"

He began to smile. The smile pulled his mouth a bit awry, but there was a pleasant taste in his mind.

It lasted till he saw the sour face of Lizzie looking out the open kitchen door.

"Late!" she said. "There never was a Finley since time begun that would be on time for his meals. There never was a one. Go on into the parlor. The school-teacher is there, up from the village. He's got something to say to you."

"You carried the word around, Lizzie?" he asked.

"Why should I waste my time?" she demanded. "I saw that gossiping old fool, Jim Sanders, driving by, and I stopped him and hollered the news to him. When he heard them, he pretty nigh fell out of his seat, but he turned his car around and drove like mad down the road. I reckon he never stopped bouncing his groceries in the back of the car till he'd told everybody. Look at here, John—was it a joke? Are you goin' to throw them all out of their houses after they get settled in?"

"It's not a joke, and I won't throw them out," said he.

"Encouraging the spendthrifts, and all," said Lizzie. "That's what I call it! But what it shows me is that you ain't any more a Finley than that rooster, there—that one with the moldy comb."

He went into the front room. A fat little man jumped up to meet him.

"Are you Mr. Witherby? I'm Tom Simpson, from the school," he said. "And I don't want to bother you any, but I've got a message to read to you. The school let out when the news came, today. There was a good deal of singing and shouting, Mr. Witherby. I guess I shouted as loud as the next man. The Simpsons used to have a place—that was thirty years ago, I guess, since my grandfather lost it. But—I have something to read to you, sir. When I called on some of my neighbors they thought we ought to send you something like this!"

He got out his glasses with nervous fingers, placed them on his nose, and then pulled a folded paper from his pocket. This he straightened, smoothed, and began:

"We, the undersigned, in token of the extreme generosity shown to us by John Witherby, and returning—"

"That's enough," said Witherby.

"Ha!" murmured the schoolmaster. He stared over his glasses at Witherby with long-distance eyes. "Enough? I wish you would hear it all, sir."

"I don't want to hear it. I understand," said Witherby.

"But at the end," insisted the teacher, glancing again at the paper, "it says: 'may this act of unbought kindness be a lasting memorial in the minds of all of the undersigned, of their families and their friends, and a token to the world that gentleness, charity, and good-will have not died from the face of the world.'"

He lowered the paper.

"I wanted you to hear that," he said. "I think it's pretty well said. Don't you?"

Witherby said, smiling: "I never read anything better. But look here—why should people be thankful when a wrong has been righted?"

"Well, the money was loaned in every case," said Simpson. "There was a real investment. Not as great in any case as the sums that your uncle used to loan to the merchants in the city, of course. And the chances he took, and the interest he got, I dare say, were not as great. But it must have taken a great resolution on your part, Mr. Witherby, to break up the great landed estate of your uncle."

He got his glasses back into his pocket, laid the paper on the table, and added: "I didn't get all the signatures of the people who are reached by your wonderful kindness, Mr. Witherby. The others, from time to time, may drop in and wish to sign their names. That is why I clipped an extra page to the document. For my own part, thank you and God bless you, sir."

He shook the iron hand of John Witherby, who smiled on him. Mr. Simpson was in such confusion that, as he got out of the room, he spilled from under his arm one of the thick batch of exercise books which he was carrying. The book fell on its back and flopped open. Witherby picked it up and saw, on the margin of the exposed page, a schoolboy's picture of a man—two circles and straight lines for arms and legs. Under the picture was a wavy line.

It was the line that caught the eye of Witherby.

"You know the boy who owns this book?" he asked.

"Yes, sir. Certainly. Harry Wilson, just half a mile up the

road, sir. A big, rough lad, and he will be wasting his time in school, I'm afraid."

"Ask Harry if he'll come down here to see me, will you?" said Witherby.

"Certainly!" said Simpson. "He'll come running. It's the big place at the other end of those woods that the Wilson family is moving back into. I'll have him here in a moment."

The teacher left, bowing himself out of the door as though he were leaving the presence of a king.

And Witherby walked slowly out into the strong sun.

"DID YOU HEAR me telling you that you're late for eating?" demanded Lizzie Finley.

"Don't bother me," said Witherby.

"Aha!" she exclaimed. "You're sorrowin' about the lost houses and the lost land, now, are you? Well, it ain't too late to call it all a joke and throw those people out again."

"Damn the people. They're not troubling me," said he.

"It's the lost money. Aye, and that's enough to bother anyone!"

"Damn the money, too," said Witherby.

"Then it's a woman," she declared.

He said nothing.

"A young girl with a pair of eyes in her head bright enough to see the heir of Dan'l Finley. That's it."

"Be quiet, Lizzie," he commanded.

"I'm a free woman in a free country, and I'll have a free tongue," she told him.

"Go talk to the wall, then," urged he.

He sat on the great, rough stone of Joseph Finley—the huge burden which had been carried three paces in 1743.

"There was a man," said Lizzie Finley. "Not one to give away land. One to add to the old place, rather. And there's the old saying that the man that lifts that stone will find a treasure under it, John. You, there, that are a man of your hands, you ought to try yourself at it."

"I've tried it," he answered.

"Stout Joseph Finley," said the woman, "he wasn't one to try and fail and give up."

He turned his head and glared at her.

"Make a bargain with me, Lizzie."

"Aye, and maybe."

"If I can lift that stone, will you stop clacking your tongue all day long?"

"If you can lift it? Aye—if you can lift it."

He rose, took a wide stance, and laid his grasp on the stone.

He bowed his knees, worked his feet on the ground to make sure that he had a good foothold, and then began to lift. He made the effort not with a wrench, but slowly. He gave the great rock first the pull of his shoulders, the strength of the mighty cordage of his bowed back. There was a sudden popping sound. Cold wind touched his flesh and he knew that the shirt had burst under the resistless pressure.

"There you are!" cried Lizzie Finley. "You've tried and failed. Let go and try again!"

He had hardly begun to exert pressure.

But now his legs commenced to straighten. The leg lift joined that of his back and shoulders. All the blood that flowed in his body seemed to be thrusting up into his head.

There was a strong pressure behind his eyes that seemed capable of thrusting them out of their sockets.

He could not breathe. His upper lip grew numb. He could see the bright, swelling purple of his cheeks.

"Stop, John! Stop, you hear me?" screamed Lizzie Finley. "You're killing yourself!"

He was lifting with every other muscle in his body; now he added, suddenly, the full might of his arms.

A thunder-stroke seemed to explode in his brain.

"It's too much for you, John!" Lizzie was screeching. "You're killing yourself. Leave go—Joseph Finley lifted it from clean ground, and now it's bogged down—"

He was making his full effort. But now he gave his body a sudden wrench.

There was a sucking, deep sound; the rock of Joseph Finley came up from its bed.

"GREAT FATHER IN Heaven!" he heard the stunned murmur of Lizzie Finley.

But this was only the beginning.

He had lifted the stone, but Joseph Finley had carried it three steps.

Witherby carried it ten. With spraddling legs he carried the huge rock away from the door ten short paces and then let it drop.

A sharp, jutting edge of it tore away the sole of his right shoe.

He turned. He had been walking into blackness. The world was still dark, with only a faint glow of red towards the direction of the sun.

Had he, in fact, blinded himself by the bursting of some blood-vessel or of some nerve behind the eyes?

He turned. His sense of balance was gone, also. He staggered.

Then he felt a lean, strong arm cast about him and a hard shoulder rammed against his ribs.

"Lean on me," said Lizzie. "You *would* play the fool! You'd go and ruin yourself! Hang Stout Joseph Finley! He never had to pull that rock out of the ground like a tooth out of a socket. And I counted the ten steps you took with it, but three was all he could make before he sank down, and the weight of the stone rolled over his legs, and he was a worthless man from that day, they say."

The blackness vanished from the eyes of Witherby.

Then a whirling red mist disappeared, and he could see again.

"Let me be," he said. "Now I can breathe again—and see. What's in the bottom of the hole the rock had made?"

"Worms," said Lizzie Finley.

It was true. In the ragged hole which marked the old sight of the boulder, there remained only some wriggling earth-worms.

18

SYMBOLS OF FORTUNE

HE WASHED HIS face and hands. The swelling was passing out of his face. His hands commenced to tremble a little. By degrees the feeling returned to his fingers.

"How would the bones of a man stand up to the strain?" asked Lizzie Finley. "Sit down to the table, now. Or would you lie down first, for a spell?"

"Nonsense," said he, huddling back into his coat. "I'm as right as can be. Is there any whisky in this damned house?"

"There's some corn whisky and there's some rum," she said.

"Rum? Let the whisky go and give me some rum, will you?"

She brought rum to him at the table, a gallon jar of it nearly full.

"Lemon juice with it, and hot water and sugar?" she asked.

He looked blankly at her.

"Why spoil it?" he said.

He picked the jar up by its small earthenware handle and filled a good glass with the liquor.

"Here's to you, Lizzie," he said, and drained the stuff to the last drop.

"Water, John?" she asked.

He smiled at her. The cold in his throat and the heat in his stomach pleased him. A wave of hot fumes swept up into his brain, and he welcomed the old sensation.

He poured another glass, but took only half of it in a large swallow.

"And yet there's them that say there's no true Finley blood in you!" said Lizzie.

"Who says that?"

"Everybody's saying it. But they'll say it no longer, now! Finley to the hair of your head and the ends of your toes!" she declared. "The good, wild Finley, all through you. There's no more Witherby in you than there is in that chair!"

She threw back her head. "I'll be having them know it, too. You've got your taste for rum, have you? All the real Finleys had the same. Jamaica rum, straight, uncut. That was their drinking. They were men. They were real men. And *you're* a man, John. I've half a heart to kiss you."

He grinned at the ugly, excited face of the harridan.

"Kiss me, then, Lizzie," he said, and lifted his head.

"Wipe your dirty, sweating face," said Lizzie.

But she did not wait for him. She took a clean corner of her apron and wiped his mouth and smacked him loudly a moment after.

"There, now," said Lizzie. "I feel better, now." She stepped back from him. "I feel as though I had some kith and kin in the house, once more. Joseph Finley—bah—he was nothing! I've tried to make a picture of him in my eye all of these years. I never threw dishwater out of that kitchen door without wondering what manner of man Joseph Finley might have been. But what do I care about him now? Not a snap of my old fingers!"

She smiled on Witherby.

"Rum, too!" she said. "Rum to make the blood richer. It was rum that Jacob and Walter Finley were drinking, those eighty years ago, when they sat right at this table and then stood up to fight."

"How did the fight go?"

"It was Jacob's hands in Walter's throat, strangling him. And strangle he did, too. And a good job, too. Because Walter had a knife out, stabbing. There's one mark he left in the table when he missed his mark."

She showed a deep gash in the wood. Time had smoothed the edges of the cut.

"Walter got his knife into the heart of Jacob. But Walter died, before ever he could catch a breath. I guess his windpipe was smashed to bits!"

She fumbled at her throat.

"There've been real men in this house before you, John," she concluded.

He fell into a deep muse while he ate his dinner. The ache of the great effort was still in the small of his back and up the tendons of his legs. But the strength of the rum kept up in his mind a pleasant noise like the humming of telegraph wires.

And in his thoughts there moved the feeling that he had taken violent possession of his own. He had laid his hands on his real life and he would carry on where the Finleys had left off—with certain old wrongs righted.

He was drinking his coffee when Lizzie came in.

"D'you know the treasure that was left under that stone you pulled out of the ground?" she asked.

He sipped coffee and sandwiched in between a taste of rum.

"Tell me, Lizzie," said he.

"In the bottom of the hole I saw the words: 'Start from Powhassett.'"

"Aye," said Witherby. "I've seen those words—and you know where."

"You thought they meant the river or the mountain?"

"Of course. What else?"

"It's fifty years since they stopped calling the Old Farm by its right name. Powhassett is what the place was called before. And what would a dying man remember except the old name?"

She grinned at him, straightened, and walked suddenly back into the kitchen.

His mind came alive. A mountain or a river—that would make a hard starting point to decipher. But the farm? It must mean the farmhouse itself, and that was a different matter.

Old Daniel Finley's body lay dead in the cellar of the house; his ghost would supervise the new search for the treasure. A sudden surety of success came over Witherby.

"Here's the lad at the door," said Lizzie. "Here's that Wilson boy that says you been asking for him."

"Send him in," said Witherby.

And in the doorway presently appeared a stout lad in overalls—the same one who had ridden past Witherby on the road, that first day, and failed to answer his questions.

Cherry knelt at the edge of the hole. "We're wrong," she said. "This isn't the place!"

Perhaps it was memory of that occasion which made Harry Wilson blush a bright scarlet, now.

"Good day, sir," he said.

"Hello, Harry," said Witherby. "Come here and sit down. I want to ask you some questions. Will you be answering, today?"

"I didn't know who you were," said Harry, miserably. "I didn't guess. Nobody guessed, at first!"

He sat down, awkwardly, in the chair beside Witherby, who took out pen and paper and drew a wavy line.

"What's that?" he asked.

"I dunno, sir," said Harry.

"Ever make a line like that?"

"No, sir."

"I saw one in your exercise book."

"Yeah. I remember. But—"

"A man standing over a line like this."

"That was an Injun," said Harry. "And he wasn't standing over it. He was standin' beside a river."

"That's a river, is it?"

"Yes, sir."

"What's this?"

He drew two short, upright lines, with a diagonal line connecting them.

"That's a gate, Mr. Finley—Witherby, I mean, sir."

"And this?"

"That's a fence."

He went on through all the symbols. The circle with a straight line under it was a tree—a round-headed tree. The upright arrow with the double head was a pine tree. The triple high zigzag lines meant three hills.

"Now this," he asked, at last. And he made the cross.

"That, sir? That's a plus, I guess."

Witherby shook his head. "In pictures, what would it be?"

The boy strained his eyes towards the ceiling. Then he shook his head.

"I'm trying like sixty," he said, "but I can't make it out."

"Give it up?"

"I gotta give it up."

"All right," said Witherby. "I won't keep you any longer."

Harry Wilson stood up from his chair. He stood straight. Thrice he blinked and swallowed like a fish.

"Outside," said Harry, blushing and hesitating, "outside, I seen the stone. I—I was wondering how it was moved, sir?"

"I moved it," said Witherby.

"You? With your own hands, sir?"

"That's right."

"My—jumping jiminy!" gasped the boy, and fled suddenly from the room.

The kitchen door slammed, and the running footfalls of the boy raced past the house. The news he carried was almost as important, perhaps, as that act of charity which had restored twenty families to their homesteads on the morning of this day.

But Witherby could not afford to think of that. He dragged out the little tape and spread it before him. He had to hurry. He had to hurry desperately. For the Doctor and all the brains of his gang were working at the same conundrum which he was striving to solve.

19

CALL FROM THE ENEMY

WHEN A PROBLEM remains in suspense, unsolved for too long, there is always to men of action a great temptation to set themselves in motion, no matter in what direction. Witherby could endure no longer. He stripped, bathed, shaved, changed his clothes—and cleaned and reloaded the automatic. He was putting the gun into a pocket when Lizzie rapped on the door and told him that there was a caller downstairs in the parlor.

Another grateful neighbor, restored to the land? That was probably it. Witherby walked carelessly down into the front room—and found the lank form of the Doctor sprawled in a chair!

The Doctor stood up and held out his hand.

"Mighty glad to see you, John," he said.

Witherby, shutting the door behind him with his left hand, became aware by straining side-glances that there was no other person in the room. He could not believe his eyes. It must be that others lurked just outside the windows. Otherwise, how could the Doctor venture, in this manner, into the lions' den?

"No, I'm quite alone," said the Doctor. "I always know, in dealing with you, that I can trust to your honor, John."

"Honor?" said Witherby. "Honor in dealing with you? You must think that I'm the damnedest fool in the world!"

"Oh, not a bit, not a bit," said the Doctor. "Merely that you are obsessed by a strong notion of what is just and proper in all cases whatsoever."

"Tell me, Doctor—what could be more just and proper than for me to break your infernal neck?"

"An infinite amount of justice, in that. But a great deal of pain for you, before the end of the trail."

Witherby walked closer to the window and glanced out.

"No one is near. It's not that," said the Doctor. "But at the end of an hour, a dozen men will begin to march towards this house. They'll come, and they'll come fast, and they'll come from every quarter of the compass. They'll walk into this house. You might stop a section of them. You might stop two or three of the couples, but the others would surely break into the house and get at you."

"If you can walk your men into gunfire, like that, why haven't you done it before?" asked Witherby.

"That's a question to be asked. It's partly because I don't like to see blood spilled. I have to pay high for my men. I have to pay *damned* high for them when they're dead. The death duties that I have to pay are shocking, John." He sighed and shook his head. "But the payments I make to widows and orphans and brothers and sisters and old parents—these payments make more of an impression on my good fellows than anything they ever collect from me into their living hands. You can see that even thieves and murderers are hopeless sentimentalists."

"Except you, Doctor?"

"Usually, I'm the exception. But today I was moved."

"Moved?"

"I could not help thinking that it would be a sad thing, John, to put away under the earth such a glorious machine as John Witherby. I heard with a good deal of honest emotion how you had lifted the rock of Joseph Finley. And that is really why I've come here."

"Go ahead."

"You're not bored?"

"You're more interesting to me than anybody in the world," said Witherby.

"I prefer to take that as a compliment," announced the Doctor.

"Stand up and turn your face to the wall," said Witherby.

"You're going to see if I'm armed?"

"I am."

"There's no weapon on me. Not even a penknife."

And suddenly Witherby knew that it was true. He sat down and stared at his visitor.

"THANK YOU," SAID the Doctor. "You're an amiable fellow, John. Too amiable for my purposes, in fact. And clever, also. I never heard of anything more clever than your return of land and houses to the yokels."

"Was that cleverness?" asked Witherby.

"Ah, you expect me to believe that it's remorse and pity? Tardy justice? But, my dear boy, I saw through your scheme at once. You knew that I had a mob against you. You wanted a mob of your own at any price. You've equipped yourself, now, with a couple of scores of men of fighting blood, all ready to die for you. If you stamp your foot the country-side rises to defend you, to follow you. A very clever move.

And what is the value of a few old farms compared with two million dollars?"

Witherby shrugged his shoulders.

"I can see," said the Doctor, continuing, "that the hunt for the treasure will be complicated for you by the fact that my men will be on the ground all the time. For me it will be complicated for the same reason. You can have watchers on the spot at all times."

He rubbed both hands over his face, and sighed. He continued almost wearily: "The thing for us to do is to throw in together, John. Don't you see that? We'll throw in together, hunt peacefully, side by side, for the treasure, and when we find it we'll divide it equally. Doesn't that make sense to you?"

"It makes a sort of sense," said Witherby."

"Good!" said the Doctor. "Besides, both for you and for me, there is a great deal of ground to cover in making the solution of the problem. Of course, by this time, you've learned that 'a start from Powhassett' meant a start from the Old Farm."

Witherby jerked up his head. The Doctor smiled at him.

"Furthermore, the rest of it follows smoothly along—go towards the three hills, come to the creek, take the creek road down to the bridge, where the arrow means that we must turn to the right, over the bridge. Then we come to a fence, and pass through the gate in the fence, and so enter the forest, the pine wood; and following in a straight line we come to a round-headed tree—a big, old oak, in fact; and then we go left again, where we come to—the cross over the figure nine! We've solved the thing to that point.

But the cross over nine—what could that mean? Of course, that's where you're also stuck."

Witherby said: "What could have persuaded the old man to string out the key on a piece of measuring tape, like that?"

"What could be a better way?" answered the Doctor. "Bits of paper and even notebooks are always being lost. But a tape like that can be kept safely in a vest pocket. Daniel Finley rarely made mistakes. He made no mistake this time—except that he died one breath too soon. However, you and I will remedy that defect. I have ideas, my boy."

"You suggest—?"

"That the two of us work together. We'll work over the ground together, you with some of your honest men; I with some of my rascals. And whatever we find we'll divide in equal shares. Do you agree?"

WITHERBY GREW ABSENT of eye for a moment. Then he said: "Finding the money is less to me than finding the murderers of my uncle. Whoever fired the bullet, Doctor, you were the brain behind the gun. I'll have nothing to do with you, except to put lead into you when I have the chance—or break your neck between my hands."

"I'm sorry you feel that way," said the Doctor.

He stood up and made no attempt to press his argument.

"I respect the integrity of your attitude," he said. "I regret what it will lead to. And now I must leave you."

"I'll have to detain you, Doctor," said Witherby.

"Will you? Think carefully, John. Realize that I would never have ventured into this house unless I had been perfectly sure of a safe return."

Witherby scowled in thought.

The Doctor went on: "To speak of other things, Cherry is a delightful girl, don't you think?"

Witherby smiled. "She's sweet poison," he agreed.

"A charming girl, and a useful girl," said the Doctor. "How rarely one finds that combination. But now I see that I am free to go, and I'm really sorry to leave you, my dear friend."

He held out his hand.

Witherby looked down at it with utter loathing.

"No, you're wrong," said the criminal. "It is the last time that we'll meet in a friendly fashion. One of us is about to die. Perhaps today, perhaps tomorrow. We ought to shake hands, John, because neither of us has ever met such a hard adversary before; and if one of us survives, he will never find such an antagonist again. Give me your hand!"

As though compelled, Witherby took the lean, cold hand of the other, and the Doctor, looking him squarely in the face, murmured: "No weakening in the end, John. I hope to see you die with a laugh."

He disengaged his hand and went straight out of the house. The door closed lightly behind him. From the window, Witherby saw the tall, spare figure striding big across the field. He snatched out a gun—he had a tight feeling in the brain, as though he were just rousing from a heavy sleep.

But he dropped the gun again into his pocket. The Doctor walked straight on, and disappeared in a clump of trees.

20

THE OLD FARM

IN THE HOT middle of the afternoon, Witherby saddled
the gray mare and rode her towards the Old Farm. He
had thought, in fact, of raising a veritable army of his new
adherents, but he dismissed the idea. It was simply his
purpose to scout over the ground; and the gray mare, he
was confident, would give him the foot over any of the
Doctor's mounted men who might be on the spot.

He carried, strapped behind the saddle, a short-handled
shovel and a pick. In his pocket there was a good electric
torch with a newly charged battery, because he felt certain
that the only safe time for him to work on the business
would be after dark. In the meantime, he was not rushed.

Instead of taking the road, he drifted the mare across
country. He never entered a copse without first scanning it
carefully; he never left it without first peering from behind
the trees across the open ground beyond. More than once
he heard voices, sounding hollow and small through the
open air, but they were almost certainly from men working in the field.

And now he came in view, from the top of a low hill, of
the Old Farm itself.

Not a living soul was in sight around the black ruins.

He looked away to north and south without finding what he wanted, but to the west there were three hills jumbled together—or rather, one hill with a treble peak. He could almost recognize it from the ragged outline of the figure on the tape. It was in that direction that he had to go.

He put the mare into a canter and headed away for the target. The hills grew out bigger and bolder. Powhassett Mountain began to look like a mountain in fact. And then he came to a small creek with a dim trail down the side of it.

That trail had been freshened a little by recent wear. He could see hoofprints left by the iron rounds of horseshoes. When he dismounted and examined the marks, he found that some of the blades of grass were still lifting, slowly—a sure proof that they had been walked on not many hours before.

The light was slanting golden out of the west, now. The air was very still. From the ground rose the slight humming of insects; and sometimes the small song of traveling wings darted past his ear and vanished in soft distance. There could not have been a time of more perfect peace, or a more peaceful scene. But he knew that this was a mask. Danger was all around him, in spite of the reassuring babble of the waters of the creek.

He mounted again and rode down the trail, now with every nerve drawn fine. Two little tributaries from the right joined the creek, swelled it to importance before he came to a humpbacked bridge over the water.

That was the bridge marked on the tape; that was the bridge which the Doctor had mentioned. He looked across it towards the fence on the other side, the old gate in the fence, the crowding small second growth pines beyond, and over the heads of them the great towering form of an oak.

The whole picture was there before him as the Doctor had mentioned it. It was very strange that the Doctor should have talked so frankly. Or did he feel that by this frankness he could win Witherby to his bargain?

The bridge looked too fragile to endure the weight of horse and man. So Witherby took the mare into a small, dense growth of poplars and tethered her there. She hung her head at once and half closed her eyes, resigned to waiting.

Leaving her there, and carrying the pick and shovel, he now went over the bridge. It creaked and swayed a little under him. Certainly it was hardly up to the burden of a horse.

Instead of taking the way through the gate, he vaulted over the fence and went on into the wood, aiming at the oak tree. He could no longer see it. The smaller, thicker growth before him shut out the view.

The sun had dropped far into the west, by this time, rolling golden currents of fire through every gap in the trees. The trunks were gilded by the light; and a close, pungent, resinous smell filled the air.

Witherby went on with the utmost caution. The footing was bad on the slippery beds of pine needles. A hundred years or so of this little pine wood and the soil would be deepened, enriched, made capable of nourishing a growth of mighty timber.

Long before that he and the Doctor would be rotting under ground; but the two millions of Daniel Finley, if they were found, would still be circulating like blood through the world.

He heard a faint clanging sound in the distance. It stopped him short in a tiny clearing that was marked off by little cypress trees on either side.

After the clanging, he heard the dim rolling of voices. The noise of them died out. He was about to stride forward again when the voice of Cherry Larue said, just behind him: "Go on, John. They're waiting for you."

HE SNAPPED AROUND, more than half prepared to see a leveled gun in those small hands of hers. But he saw her looking very boyish in a riding outfit. Women are apt to look either baggy or scraggly in riding clothes, but she looked neither. It seemed to Witherby that he had never seen her so pretty. Perhaps it was the stock that set off her face so well. She was sleeking a riding crop through her gloved hands.

"Jack-in-the-box again, eh?" said Witherby. "If you're here trouble can't be far away."

"It isn't," said the girl. "Walk straight ahead and you'll find the Doctor and his best men. They're looking for you, too."

"Thanks," said Witherby. "I'm half believing you."

"I've never lied to you," she answered.

He laughed. "But that's all right," he told her. "The Doctor said that you'd always be able to string me along. You've done it three times. How are you going to manage to do it now? How are you going to deliver me to them, tied hand and foot?"

"Hush!" said the girl. And she lifted a hand to command his silence.

Afterwards he could hear sounds coming steadily towards him.

"Back here!" murmured the girl. And he found himself obeying her, drawing back deep into a thicket of tall saplings and brush.

Sounds of moving men came closer. He had a glimpse, through the leaves, of that lean, sallow-faced Charlie walking with others—with five others who carried picks and shovels and axes. They came out into the little clearing which the girl and Witherby had just vacated.

There, glad to be free from the underbrush through which they had been forcing, they paused for a moment.

"Where's the Doctor?" asked one.

"Gone off the other way," said Charlie.

Red-headed Ad mopped his forehead with the back of his hand. "This is a lot of work and no damn good," he said. "Are you going to dig up the whole forest? The Doctor's on a crazy lost trail."

"You ever know the Doctor to be beaten?" asked Charlie, turning on Ad.

"Yeah, I've known him beaten."

"By what?"

"By the strong man—by Witherby. That's who!"

"Witherby had luck."

"Nobody has luck three times in a row," declared Ad.

"That's a large way to talk," said Charlie, slowly.

"I mean it large," answered Ad. "The old man's slowing down. He's not what he used to be. He walked into that house today and come out, and he didn't bring anything with him, and he didn't leave anything changed behind him. He's slowing down."

"If I was a mind-reader," said Charlie, "I wouldn't pick the Doctor to start practicing on."

"There's a lot in all of this mystery," said Ad. "Hard cash spent in the right spots—that's where the Doctor buys most of his tricks."

"Maybe you could do a better job?" asked Charlie.

"Maybe I could give my men a squarer cut," declared Ad. "Here's a couple of millions in sight, somewhere— and what'll the rest of us get apiece? A couple of hundred, maybe. Maybe he'll even give us a whole grand apiece— and he hogs the rest!"

"You've got to figure your profits by the year," said Charlie. "You spent eight months of the year in jail before the Doctor picked you up."

"The four other months was sweet, though."

"Were you ever pinched since the Doctor took hold of you?"

Confronted by undeniable facts, Ad merely growled: "Ah, go to hell!"

Someone said: "Where's the girl?"

"She's around."

"The Doctor told us to pick her up," said Charlie.

"It'd take better men than any of us to pick up *that*," said one of the men.

At this, even Charlie laughed a little.

"She can take care of herself, all right," he admitted at last.

And they walked on through the brush again.

21

INTO THE TRAP

A DEEP, STILL, swelling sense of wonder possessed Witherby. He pulled out a handkerchief and wiped the wet from his face.

"What's the matter with you?" he asked the girl. "One word—and the game was off, as far as I'm concerned. I never could have got away."

She smiled up at him.

"It's because the Doctor doesn't want me dead, now? Is that it?" asked Witherby. "He's troubled about his treasure hunt and he thinks that I may know a little more than he does?"

She kept on smiling.

"Talk to me, Cherry," he commanded. "I'm getting nervous."

"You won't be nervous long," she answered.

"What'll cure me?"

"Lead."

"I'll be dead, you mean?"

"You're asking for it, aren't you?"

"I don't know. Maybe. By walking into the woods, here?"

"That's one thing. John, the Doctor's willing to split fifty-fifty with you. Why don't you do it?"

"That's it, is it? You're to pick me up where you can and persuade me?"

"If the Doctor could find you, he'd rather have you dead than persuaded."

"He has a real hate on for me, hasn't he?"

"He has some reasons."

"Tell me a few."

"You heard that red-head talking, a minute ago?"

"I heard him."

"Ad isn't the only one who's doing some thinking of his own. There's trouble on the Doctor's hands, and he blames you for all of it."

"I'm glad he does."

"Be glad while you can."

"Cherry, what chance do you think I have of winning through?"

"One chance in a hundred thousand."

"The Doctor as good as all that?"

"You don't know him, John. You never would know him."

"Why not?"

"Because you prefer to work with your hands." She took his right hand and turned it in hers. "It doesn't look like so much of a hand after all, does it?" she said, smiling up at him again. "But you have to work with the old brain to understand the Doctor."

"You help me, then."

"That's why I'm here," she said.

"Thanks," said he. And he began to laugh at this effrontery. "I'm glad to have you on my side, Cherry."

"You won't listen to me?"

"I love listening to you. I've told you that."

"If you'll listen, I'll make you believe."

"Go right ahead, Cherry. But hurry it. It's getting on towards sunset."

Dusk was already settling through the trees. A wind came out of the west and made over their heads a sound like the rushing of mountain waters.

"You're stuck with the Doctor on one reef, aren't you?"

"Yes."

"The cross over nine?"

"That sticks me," he admitted, freely. "Tell me what that means and I'll know you're on my side, Cherry."

"It might mean to cross over nine steps—or feet—or inches," she suggested.

"Yes, but cross over what, and in what direction?"

"Have you a guess?"

"The creek, maybe. I don't know. If I did know, do you think that I'd tell you about it?"

She sighed. She poked a slender finger through a button-hole of his coat and shook her head.

"Well, what do crosses stand for?"

"Plus, perhaps. Plus nine more of something, perhaps it means."

"It isn't a plus. The horizontal line is made too near the top for that."

"That was carelessness. Uncle Daniel was not a penman."

"That cross wasn't written. It was drawn in. It was neatly made."

"Was it?" he asked.

"Yes."

"But what does that mean?"

"Simply that it's a cross, not a plus sign.

"That leaves me farther off than ever."

"But what do crosses stand for?" she asked.

"The Holy Cross, churches, things like that."

"Nothing else?"

"Not that I can think of."

"There's another meaning. People put crosses at the head of graves, don't they?"

"Yes," said he. "What of that? You mean at nine—whatever that is—the money is buried?"

"There used to be a village, out here—I don't know how many generations ago. We've found the foundations. Nothing else. The village was built of wood, and it burned, and the forest grew right over it."

"What has that to do with crosses?" he asked.

"Well, there must have been a church in the village—it was usual to have a church almost as soon as there were three houses built."

"Go on. I don't follow you at all," he confessed.

"Beside a church there would be a graveyard, wouldn't there?"

"I suppose so."

"Well, then, suppose that Uncle Daniel found the graveyard. Suppose that he buried his stuff on the ninth grave?"

"Hey!" exclaimed Witherby.

"Do you think I'm on your side now, John?"

"Have you found the graves?" he asked.

"No. I haven't wanted to find them for the Doctor. But I'd like to hunt for them with you, John."

HE HESITATED. SOMEWHERE there was a trap.

"Will the Doctor take all his men away from the place?"

"No. He'll have men around."

"We won't be able to search very carefully, then."

"Maybe not."

"Where away are the ruins?"

"The foundations of the old town? They're hard to find. The Doctor turned them up. I'll show you the way."

She turned and walked before him. He strained his eyes at her. There was still plenty of light to see her by, but he was trying to peer through her at the truth. And that he could not see.

He saw that he was walking a half stride behind her. She was leading him once more. She was leading him to what?

The woods were darkening fast, now. Danger rose like the shadow out of the ground. And as she had done to him before, so she was apt to do again. Yet he could not find it in him to stretch out a hand and stop her.

He went on with his hand on the automatic, peering earnestly to this side and that. Always he had the feeling that the enemy was gathering like a whisper behind his back, ready to leap out. When a twig snapped under his foot it sent through him a shock that reached the brain.

An instant later she lifted her hand. She stepped back and touched him, still pointing, then moved soundlessly under the arching side of a great shrub.

He, stepping beside her, saw at last what her sharper eyes had found coming through the thick of the twilight. It was a man with a rifle slung in his hand. He came out of the trees, whistling through his teeth, a barely audible sound. Before he passed the bush that sheltered the pair he paused. Then he stepped on with a noiseless footfall.

Witherby crouched. Leaping is a foolish business. It is slower than a run, and it throws a man awkwardly out of position in the air. It was for a sprinting start that he bent down. Then he hurled himself forward with one of those quick starts which football players learn. The rifleman spun about on the balls of his feet. He was a third of a second too late. The left hand of Witherby gripped the rifle. The right hand clubbed the other at the base of the jaw.

There was not a sound. The man dropped for the ground, hung with dangling body over the bent arm of Witherby, who held the rifle in his free hand.

"Take the gun, Cherry," he said to the girl.

She came quickly.

"You're through doubting, John?" she asked.

"Damn the doubting," he answered.

At that she took the rifle, and stood by while he laid the Doctor's man on the ground. He was in her hands again, but he felt a savage triumph in trusting her thus for the fourth time. Besides, there was growing up in him, once more, the miraculous flower of faith, which told him that on all the other occasions she had in fact been made to appear what she was not.

In the meantime, he pulled out cord. No one who had traveled the sea as much as John Witherby would ever be found without a few twists of twine about him. It is stronger than rope, if it is used in many windings.

With it, he lashed the ankles of the stranger, tied his wrists behind his back, tied the wrists and the ankles by another bit of the twine, and lashed the extra piece of cord around the knees of the prisoner.

THE BOUND MAN recovered himself with a groan.

"No noise," said Witherby.

The other was silent. Only his breathing was loud. Witherby motioned the girl back, but she was already almost out of sight in the brush.

"Who are you?" grunted the captive.

"John Witherby."

"Witherby? My God! Look here, Witherby—I never lifted a hand against you!"

"What's your name?"

"Sexton. Lew Sexton."

"How long have you been with the Doctor?"

"About—about a couple of years."

"Then I ought to break your neck. But I may not if you'll talk out to me."

"Try me!" said Sexton, fervently.

"How long were you to keep this beat?"

"About three hours."

"Anybody else on watch with you?"

"No. Not exactly."

"How do you mean—not exactly?"

"There's two more. Sam and Cruiser. They're to go the rounds about every hour and a half and find me, and see what I've got to say. See that I'm awake, too, I suppose."

"Where were they to find you?"

"Anywhere around here."

"Do they signal you?"

"They whistle, like this—"

"Never mind!"

"Two low whistles, with a pause between them."

"Sexton, I hate to gag a man."

"God knows I hate to be gagged—and choke on it."

"I'll tell you what I'll do. I'll fix a gag that won't be a gag at all. But you can hold it between your teeth. When you want to get rid of it, you can do that. But if they find you, it'll look as if you had no chance to shout for help."

"Partner, you're a white man," gasped Sexton.

And, taking the handkerchief out of the pocket of the prisoner, Witherby made the false gag and bound it with a cord that went around the head of the captive.

"Can you breathe?" he asked, anxiously.

"I can breathe fine. More power to you," said Sexton. "If I had the doing of things over again—"

Witherby turned from him and went to the girl.

22

CITY OF THE DEAD

SHE WAS SO thoroughly browned that her face seemed as dark as that of a Negro, in this light. But he could see the flash of her eyes and her smile.

"He's not badly hurt?" she said.

"He'll be all right."

"It was Sexton," she said.

"What sort of a fellow?"

"Murder," she said.

He hesitated, about to go back and cinch up the gag. But he finally shrugged his shoulders. That was his greatest fault—he was too apt to take chances.

"I left him with a thing that don't really mean a gag," he said. "But I hate to half choke a poor devil."

"He's choked others," she commented. "And with his hands, too. Sexton is the blackest of the lot."

"Well, let him go," said Witherby.

He pulled out his electric torch. When he touched the switch the light slid over the ground, making one bright halfmoon on the pine needles not far before them and then spreading in a wide, dim cone.

"This way," said the girl.

He turned the light, suddenly, straight into her face. She gasped and then shook her head at him.

"That's not fair, John," she said.

"No. It was a rotten thing to do," he agreed. "But—there's a crazy jumping in my nerves. I'm trying to forget anything that ever happened in the past between us."

"Why?" she asked, as the light swung away from her. "We've had some pretty high minutes, between the first and the last. This way, John."

She was leading the way, again, while he followed with the pick and the shovel in the grasp of his hand. He had given her the light to carry now. He felt that she was the brains and he the mere laborer of the party.

Twice she paused, once to listen carefully; once to show him the exposed foundation of a house.

"The Doctor dug it up for the fun of the thing. He's losing his grip or he wouldn't leave signs like that behind him."

He listened to this comment with a curious interest.

"If you were leading a gang of thugs, you wouldn't do foolish things like that, would you, Cherry?" he asked.

She laughed a little, and went on without a reply. But he was trouble deep in his mind. She was not like other people. Certainly she was not like other girls of her age.

He said, as they went slowly on through the trees: "I want to hear everything, before long. Everything about how you came to hitch up with the Doctor."

"Sometime I'll tell you everything," she answered carelessly. "But we've another job on our hands now, John. Look—you see the mounds?"

She swung the light behind her. For his own part, he

could make out little except the trees and the crossing shadows of the trunks.

"We're following the line of the old street, all right," she said. "It's like walking underground, don't you think?"

The grisly idea did not please him.

"Think of something better than that," he suggested.

She laughed again. Her laughter was no more than a whisper, and yet there was real merriment in it. "You're not a poet, whatever you are," she said.

And she took the lead again.

She stopped at a point where the trees stood thicker than ever.

"This might be the place," she said.

"What place?"

"The graveyard. The trees are bigger here. They didn't have to find their rootage among the foundations. Look under the trees with me."

They moved forward slowly, she swinging the light from side to side.

"There!" exclaimed the girl, suddenly. And she pointed.

"What is it?"

"Don't you see?"

"Pine needles and tree trunks. That's all."

"You're looking for something too big. Of course the soil would have settled almost entirely, in all of these years. But—there—and there—don't you see the little mounds?"

He could see them, after they had been pointed out. There was a regular row of them. He counted four; and then two tree trunks, standing close together, cut out the view of the rest of the line.

"This is the place!" she said.

SHE WAVED HER hand.

"The church must have stood off there. This is the grave-yard. And here are the graves, John!" she said. "See how they're laid out, regularly, as if the dead bodies were planted to grow."

There was something almost ghoulish to him, in her excitement. He had forgotten, well nigh, the cause that had brought them here. But she was as keen as a ferret.

She was carrying on her exploration rapidly and seriously. He blundered after her, seeing more with his mind than with his eyes, and what he was seeing was the character of the girl. What could he make of all these contradictions?

"Here!" she said. "See how it clears up! They didn't scatter their dead all over the churchyard. They laid them out in good order—like seeds from a drill. You see? Here the graves stop. This little mound, here, seems to be the last—this one with the tree growing out of the end of it. Here lies Aunt Mary, or Grandma Margaret, or Sister Mary, or Uncle Charlie, or my late beloved husband, John."

"Quit it, Cherry, will you?" he exclaimed.

"Hush! Not so loud!" she warned him. And she began to laugh. "Why should we be sorry for people in heaven?" she asked.

His spirit was depressed.

"There's a meaning to that cross over nine," she said. "Take my word for it, it means the ninth grave."

"The ninth out of fifty, say? Where would we begin counting?"

"At the head of that first long row of mounds. Find the first one we struck and then count up to nine—and dig!"

He went back with her. They numbered off the low mounds. Out of the fifth one, as he had seen before, grew two trees. But there were others beyond. They counted the seventh, the eighth. They came to the ninth mound, and he struck his pick into the soil.

She stood back, shining the torch on the work, silent. And he was glad of the silence, because it enabled him to use his thoughts for things other than his work. He tore up great chunks of the sod with the pick. Some with his hands, some with his shovel he cleaned away. He began to sink the pick in again, to dig out another level of the earth. What was this girl? His mind kept asking the question. Impersonal, almost obscenely impersonal, he felt.

"Wait a minute, John," she said.

He suspended the pick. She kneeled on the edge of the hole he had dug, peering.

"We're wrong," she said calmly. "This isn't the place!"

23

THE SIGNAL

HE HARDLY CARED about the bad news. It seemed to him that the finding of the great buried treasure of Daniel Finley was far less important than the truth about this girl, if only he could mine it out of her. But how was he to get at it?

She was saying: "You see how that soil is all compacted? No one has disturbed it for a long time. Notice how the little roots grow right through, close under the surface? That shows that no one has dug here for a long time."

He leaned on the pick and looked grimly down at the ground. He could not fathom his own abstraction. It was insane for him to feel so divorced from this proceeding. Was it not his own money that he was digging for?

She stood up. "Now, then, what next?" she asked.

"Nothing next. We'll have to go home and do some thinking and come back here—"

"Hush!" she said. "We'll never have such a chance as this to come back. Do you think the Doctor will ever again leave this ground under such a light guard?"

"I can bring fifty men and camp them on the place," he suggested.

"Don't bother me, John. I want to think. I was sure—I could have sworn—"

She turned out the light. He could hear rather than see her walking up and down a few paces this way and that. He lifted his head and saw, towards the west, the last bronze sheen of the sky, copper and green intermingling.

"So!" said Cherry Larue. "Now my poor old brain begins to work again. There's another end to the line of graves, of course. We'll try to find that end. Come on, John!"

She went before him with her quick steps. Right up the line of the graves they went.

"Here!" she said, halting. "This seems to be the last one. It *is* the last one. You see those old, moldering stones? That must be all that's left of the wall that once went around the graveyard. This is the last grave. Now begin with me, and count them back."

They counted back nine and paused on another mound. At once she began to kick the pine needles away from the top of the soil. Then she stood back. Her torch twisted up in her hand. The light stood for an instant like a tall, white ghost in the foliage of a tree. Then it switched down and illumined the ground for him.

At the first stroke of the pick there was a difference. The pick sank in right up to the haft.

"We've got it!" cried Cherry Larue. "That ground has been moved not so long ago. Dig, John, dig!"

"*We're* going to win," he corrected her, and tore into the ground with the pick again.

He discarded the pick. It was not necessary in ground of this consistency. He took the short-handled shovel and wielded it with the might of his swinging shoulders. The flying loads of earth landed in a regular pulsation of thudding sounds. He did not look up. Down a foot, two feet, three feet he sank the hole, and then nearly tore the shovel from his hands by striking the edge of it against something tough. A root?

That would mean that they were wrong again.

He scraped some of the earth away, drove his hand into the loose soil, and felt between his fingers the tough texture of a tarpaulin. He straightened.

"It's here," he said, quietly.

"Ah, ah!" gasped the girl. And her body lightened suddenly. She was standing on tiptoe.

He snatched the light from her and shone it in her face.

"Why in hell do you care so much for money?" he demanded.

"Because I'm human," she answered. "Take the light away, John."

"You're going to marry me, Cherry?"

"Of course I am. If I can wangle it, I'm certainly going to marry you, John." She began to laugh, joyously. And his mind darkened.

"Aye," he said. "Two million dollars will sweeten the best husband in the world, I'd say."

"Of course it will," she answered, frankly. "When we go to Paris, a whole lot of the Rue de la Paix will stick to my fingers. Dig, John. Let's see what's there. Why do you keep worrying about me? No matter how bad I may be, I'm the girl you're going to have. You know that, John. Why do you keep doubting me, when the doubting won't keep you from buying a marriage license?"

HE TURNED GRIMLY back to his work. It was true. No

matter how he revolted, he knew that he had to have her, at any price. The world, without her, would be a world of starvation, to him.

He scraped the earth away still more. He laid his grip on the tarpaulin and pulled. There was a tearing sound.

"Loosen more ground, or you'll tear it to pieces, John!" she urged.

Then, from not far away, he heard a whistle. A pause, and the whistle repeated.

"What is it?" asked the girl.

"The Doctor's men. Looking for Sexton. Two of them looking for Sexton."

"Then—work fast—work with your hands, John!" commanded her whisper.

That was the idea, of course. The shovel would make too much noise. She had snapped out the torch at the first sound they heard. In darkness he kneeled in the hole in the ground, and began to work loose the soil around the tarpaulin, digging deep with his powerful fingers.

He paused. A light flashed through the trees. He saw the white sheen of it on the face of the girl. Then she dropped to the ground beside him. He could feel the weight of her shoulder. He could feel the tremor of her body, and hear the irregular, fast breathing.

Footsteps were coming.

"What one of the boys was digging around here?" asked Charlie.

"Why?"

"I just stumbled over some loose ground."

How far had he flung that infernal soil with the swinging shovel?

A light flashed beyond a thick shrub. Rays, slices, sharp arrows of the light broke through the bush and struck at the girl and big John Witherby. He had the automatic in his hand with the safety catch slipped.

"Somebody's been digging, all right," said the voice of Ad. "Take a look."

"What for?" answered Charlie. "If anything had been found, wouldn't we have known about it?"

"Not if the chief had a chance to do the thing by himself. He'd like nothing better than a chance to scoop the lot of us. I'm going to take a look."

"Take a look and be damned. I'm going on to find that Sexton. The wooden-head's asleep somewhere around here."

Steps moved on.

"Well," drawled Ad, "I suppose you're right," and his footfall went noisily after Charlie.

The sounds died.

"That was a near one," murmured the girl. "And think of Charlie making the slip—Charlie, with a brain almost as good as the Doctor's! There's luck with us tonight, old boy!"

He was already digging. The tough ground parted under his powerful fingers, he could reach well down the side of the bulky tarpaulin, now, and finally he brought it out with a last strong pull.

"There it is," he said.

Thirty pounds. That was all there was to the thing. How could a thirty-pound weight be worth a couple of millions?

"Is that all?" she murmured.

She flashed the torch into the hole that he had made. It

showed the compacted earth at the bottom of the cavity and through the earth a crooked veining of little roots.

"That's the bottom," she said. "We've cleaned it out— and now we're away."

The whistle was repeating in the near distance. Suddenly a voice answered with a great shout.

"They've got to Sexton," he said. "That means they'll be hot-footing it after us as fast as they can—"

He had hardly spoken before three shots sounded, in rapid succession.

"Are the fools fighting each other?" muttered big John Witherby, as he picked up the sack.

"No, no!" gasped the girl. "It's a signal. Pray God it doesn't surround the place with men. Quick, John. We'll go straight on—away from the Old Farm. Trouble is only starting for us, now!"

24

BAYING PURSUIT

AGAIN, BEHIND THEM, and again the three shots were fired in close succession.

They could hear other sounds—the far beating of the hoofs of horses, and then the baying of dogs.

They were hurrying forward, he with the tarpaulin in his hand, jogging with a long, easy stride, the girl sprinting to keep up. But now he paused with a jerk.

"What's that?" he snarled.

"It means they're gathering, John! What else?" she breathed.

"The dogs—the damned dogs—has the Doctor got hounds that will follow a trail?" he demanded.

"Yes. But we'll get to the river—we'll get water between us and the dogs. And then—"

He groaned.

"Take a grip on the pocket on my coat and hold hard. We've got to move," he commanded, and straightway, he broke into a hard run. She kept up valiantly for a few moments. Then he could feel her weight pulling back on him, slewing him around a little.

"John, stop," she called.

The pressure of her hand stopped. He paused, gasping: "Come on, Cherry! Are you all in? I'll carry you, by God—"

"Go on!" she said. "I'll fade out. There's no use in my staying with you—"

"There is—Cherry, don't talk like a fool. If the Doctor dreams that you've thrown in with me—and he'll find your trail beside my trail—he'll strangle you with his own hands—come on!"

At that moment, the far, ringing chorus of many deep-throated hounds commenced.

"They've found the start! Come on, Cherry," he shouted.

She caught her hand in his pocket once more, and again they fled forward, and rounded the top of a hill. Below, with a dim, oily shining, they marked the face of the river. The moon was not yet up. In the still places along the banks they could see the shuddering images of the stars.

The baying of the dogs was growing stronger through the woods behind them as they reached the edge of the water.

"Stay here with the tarpaulin," he directed. "There's nothing on this side, but there's a boat over there, you see?"

A hundred feet of water separated him from the craft. He tore off shoes and coat, ran up the bank a few steps, and with a running start hurled himself into the water—a racing dive in which he smacked the river with almost the full length of his body. Then, with churning feet, with reaching arms, he drove through the stream.

It had looked almost flat; but he was hardly out from the shore before he felt the current taking hold. He would have to land far below the boat, at the rate the stream was taking him.

*Over the brow of
the hill he saw
shadows streaming*

Once he looked back over his shoulder and saw the dim silhouette of the girl, standing on the shore. She looked small as a child.

It had been her brain work that had placed the treasure in their hands. It had been her work, and hers only, and she had barely completed it in time.

His down sweeping hand touched mud. He stood up and staggered through the remainder of the stream. The boat was above him, to the left. He ran up to it and found that it was padlocked to a pile driven into the mud of the bank. One powerful wrench, and he had pulled out the staple that held the padlock in place.

He leaped into the water up to his waist, lifted the little skiff, and whirled it around so that the bow was pointing in the right direction. He lifted himself into the craft, snatched up the oars, made them bend to the breaking point against the tholes. Each stroke forced the boat to leap away—and then, over the brow of the hill, he heard the outcry of the hounds pour suddenly down at him.

He strained his head over one shoulder. He could see the girl where she had been before. No, she had wisely moved down the stream a little so that he could use the force of the downward current instead of trying to cut straight across it.

But now, over the brow of the hill, he saw the hunt streaming, shadowy silhouettes against the stars, with the low-running dogs in front and eight or nine horsemen sweeping in the rear. He could hear the loud yell that told him the men had sighted the girl by the water.

And he? He was too late!

Three times more he swept at the oars, mightily, but as he turned he could see that the forefront of the riders had overtaken the dogs, scattering them, sweeping forward toward the girl.

Why did she not run?

She could see that the boat would never get to her. Half the width of the current still separated him from the shore. And guns were beginning. Bullets hit the water all around him with dim white leapings of spray. Bullets drove through the frail sides of the boat. They went through with light, drum-beat sounds.

HE HAD TO lie down. Over the edge of the gunwale, as the boat began to whirl slowly in the current, shooting down in the strength of the water, he saw the whole mob break around the girl:

The Doctor's voice yelled above the rest: "Get him! Ten thousand dollars to the first man to find another boat—ten thousand to the man who puts a slug through the head of Witherby!"

And then, distinctly, he could make out the shrill, sweet voice of the girl, crying: "What do you care about him? Here's the Finley money! Chief, do you see the tarpaulin?"

"By God, is that true?" cried the Doctor. And a wild cheer went up from them, while the dogs ran down the edge of the water, howling at the little boat that carried Witherby farther and farther away.

They would have discovered what was in the tarpaulin sooner or later—but why had she not run with it, when she saw the hunt coming? Why had she not broken away into the brush, where they might have hunted her vainly until moonrise, at least!

Aye, or longer. And with her craft, her subtlety, she might have gotten away completely!

As it was, the game was lost. He had on his hands perhaps enough money in the bank to permit him to pay his inheritance tax. The majority of the land of the great farm had been returned to the dispossessed owners. And he was little better than a poor man himself—while in the Doctor's hands lay the fortune which the cruel brains and the patience of Daniel Finley had heaped together.

Two million dollars?

It seemed to Witherby that two million damnations were heaped on his burning head at this moment.

He sat up. They would remember him, in spite of the money, before long.

He pulled the oars strongly for the farther side of the river, and towards the east he saw a pyramid of fire mounting above the trees.

The pyramid dissolved into a greater, rounder brilliance. And then the thin edge of the moon was gleaming at him above the trees. The pines seemed to be gathered in a mist of pale fire. They seemed to be burning.

The point of the bow struck soft mud. He sprang from the boat onto the shore, and pulled the skiff up after him. And at the sight of this maneuver, as though they realized that he was passing beyond their ken, the dogs raised a great howling on the bank.

But no riders had followed the course of the boat. He was left to his own devices, as though in utter scorn.

And why not? They had won the game. They had won the great prize. With such loot as this on hand, the Doctor would probably break up his old formation and disappear from this section of the country. In some cheerful capital of Europe, he would settle down to the wise investment and the joyous spending of his stolen money while John Witherby, before long, would be out again in the world, with no riches greater than the strength of his hands.

And the girl?

He clamped his teeth shut. They could have the money and be damned with it. But he would get to Cherry Larue, in one way or another.

He sat down, with the black shadow of some tall shrubs falling over him. He saw the gleaming face of the river brighten as the moon climbed higher. Soon the water was flashing with a thousand brilliant facets. Up the farther shore, as the moon rose, he could clearly see the busy group of people all huddled together about a common center, while the loosed horses began to graze here and there on the cool grass.

He knew what that center was. They were opening the

tarpaulin. He prayed that they might find nothing but worthless stones inside it.

But a great yell came tingling down to him, now. He could see, dimly, the brandishing of arms high in the air. And he knew that all the expectation of the thieves had been justified by their discoveries inside the packet.

25

"MURDER'S NO GOOD!"

HE HAD TO get across the river to them. He had to get across to the treasure, to the girl, and to the Doctor. Almost above all, he had to reach the Doctor.

Because, as Witherby kneeled there in the shadow of the brush, a strange, still, cold, deep conviction was breeding in him. He had done many unworthy things in his life. He had defiled himself more than once with bad actions, with liquor, with almost all that a man can do; and now it seemed to him that there was one way in which he could wash himself clean and undo the past.

He could kill the Doctor. He could remove that grisly menace from the earth, and somehow he would manage it.

He was half rising, prepared to go before he knew how he could cross the river safely.

It occurred to him that he could slip soundlessly into the water and swim to the farther side. Then he realized that this would be useless. There were too many of them and they would shoot too straight. He could see his goal, but he could not reach it. If he fired, he could not be certain of striking the Doctor in that huddle of bodies, in the moon-light. Besides, the girl was constantly close to the side of the Doctor, as though in fact she wanted to protect him or share his dangers.

Then Witherby realized that hanging trembling on his mark, like a bull terrier in an agony of desire for the fight, would accomplish nothing. He would have to get at the Doctor in another way. And that way would be not by trailing through the woods but by striking on another field. He was one against many. Some element of surprise would be needed to equalize the odds. And how could he take the Doctor by surprise?

There was one place where the Doctor would never expect to see him again. That was at 112 East Fifteenth Street. And that was where Witherby must try to see him again—simply because he knew how impregnable the place was, and because the Doctor knew he knew it. The thought of going back to that house of danger struck him sick, it made him breathe small, but he knew that he would have to make the attempt, at least.

So he went back, slowly, through the brush. He struck off at a steady dog trot that devoured the ground. Up the side of the river he went. A creek cut in from the right. He waded it. It was up to his chin, in the center, and cold as ice. He went on. His socks were worn out to tatters. His feet were cut on the edge of a stone, now and then. But that made no difference.

He crossed another creek. The round sweep of the river had been covered, now. It had diminished. He saw the humped back of the bridge. And in another moment he was with the gray mare.

She had lain down, patiently, her head lifted high by the tethering reins. He untied them and she stood up. She whinnied a little and nuzzled his shoulder. And he went swiftly home on her back, running her hard across the fields, winging her across the fences.

When he came to the old Finley house, it fitted into his mind like a familiar face. It had a greeting for him, as though the soul of Daniel Finley realized that a true avenger had come to put things right. The Doctor had to die. He had to die for the sake of the world; he had to die for the sake of Daniel Finley's ghost.

A lamp burned in the kitchen. There was no other light.

He took the mare to the watering trough, let her drink, gave her a feed of grain in the barn. When he went out, she stopped hogging her oats and whinnied after him again.

That made him smile as he hobbled on his sore feet to the house. As he turned the knob of the kitchen door, the voice of Lizzie Finley snarled: "Late again! Late again! There never was a true Finley that didn't waste the time of the cook, and set down to a cold meal! If ever—"

He had the door open, now, and the sight of him struck the last words from her mouth. She looked from his tousled hair down to his bleeding feet. Then she strode before him to his room.

Without a word she started his bath water running. She laid out fresh clothes for him, and a pair of shoes. Still without speaking, she left the room.

He bathed, dressed, went down to the table. His feet hurt him rather badly. Well, he was apt to have to endure worse pains than these before the night ended.

Lizzie served him carefully, keeping her eyes on the food, never on his face, and he kept silence until he reached coffee.

"Sit down," he said to Lizzie Finley, then.

She sat down at the end of the table. He studied her hard face as he sipped his second cup of coffee.

She surprised him by saying: "Don't do it, John!"

"Don't do what?" he asked.

"The thing that makes you keep gripping your jaws so hard. Besides, murder's no good."

He stared at her.

"I know the Finley," she went on.

"There's something that needs doing," he told her. "First, get me a sheet of paper."

She brought him a writing pad. He wrote on it, under the date: "I, John Witherby, being in full possession of my faculties, and fearing that I am about to die, do will and bequeath all my properties to Elizabeth Finley. If I have disappeared and do not return within five days, the estate becomes hers."

HE SIGNED THIS document and passed it across the table to the cook. She read it and uttered no exclamation. Only, very slowly, she lifted her eyes to his.

"I don't know any other Finley," he said.

"You're the one, are you?" said she. "You're the one that Uncle Dan'l is to pull down after him? Well, I wouldn't be surprised. Stout Joseph Finley, he dropped the rock on his legs, and he never was a man afterwards. And after this night, I reckon you'll be cold enough to put under ground, John. Have some more coffee?"

He nodded. She went out into the kitchen and returned. She filled his cup, pouring the brown-black stream through a strainer.

"You know, John, you could lead a pretty good life here."

"Yes," he said.

"Even if you been and missed some of the things that Dan'l left for you, you could lead a pretty good life with what's left."

"Yes," he nodded.

"There's them that love you. There's people living all around, now, that love you. It's the first time, I reckon, that so many folks ever loved a Finley!"

He only smiled at her.

"Is there a girl in it?"

"Yes," he said.

"What sort of a girl might she be?"

"She's not beautiful—not very," he answered, judiciously.

"Is she in your blood or in your head?"

"She's in my blood."

"When you think of her, does everything inside of you give a leap?"

"Yes," said he.

"Then there's no good talking," said Lizzie Finley.

"There's no good talking," he agreed.

"Once I was that way," she went on, brooding. "He wasn't so much of a man, neither. He was kind of soft-looking. He even had a small voice. But when he looked at me, something like a scare went through me. I wouldn't see him. I thought I was scared. But I was wrong. After he went away, I seen how wrong I'd been. He wrote me a letter. It was such a nice letter to say good-by that I felt that I'd be a fool if I wrote back and told him that he didn't need to say good-by."

After this, she made a pause.

"I'm sorry about that," said Witherby.

"Aye," said she, "you'd be sorry. You're the kind that would be sorry for other folks. There's too much heart in you. Not enough brains. There never was another Finley like you. But if there'd been some of your spirit in him, he wouldn't never of let it go at the writing of a letter. But he didn't have anything of John Witherby in him. He wouldn't go out to risk his neck for a girl, the way you're going to do."

"Not for the girl. But because Uncle Daniel was murdered, Lizzie—and because I know the man who has to die for it."

"Is that it?"

"Yes. That's it."

"There ain't any money about it?"

"None that I'll get my hands on. The money's gone."

"Ha!" grunted Lizzie. The shock of that news made her blink. "The others—they found the money?"

"I found it. But they got it away."

"Away from you? They never did! You'd of died, first."

"Never mind how. They got it away."

In the silence that followed, he could see her straightening more and more.

"How the ghost of Uncle Dan'l must be turnin' and groanin' in the grave!" she whispered.

"I suppose it is," he answered.

"And where does the girl come into all of this?"

"She comes in—afterwards."

At this, Lizzie began to nod in a deep understanding.

"With a real man, the work comes first, and the women, they come afterwards," she said.

"I think so," said he.

She got up from her chair and went suddenly into the kitchen. He, for his part, finished the coffee without haste.

She brought in the jug of rum, unasked. He took one glass of it, sipping it slowly. She was back in the kitchen again when he stood up and left the house. As he went through the kitchen he held out his hand.

"Good-by, Lizzie," he said.

She took the hand in her cold, bony grasp.

"God keep and help you," she said.

"Maybe He will," said Witherby, seriously.

He turned away, quickly. She followed him and held the door open. The shaft of light struck out straight towards the barn, though it was too dim to be noticeable when he reached the door of the stable. But it seemed to him that the spirit of the old woman was striding along with him, giving strength and comfort.

When he rode out on the gray mare, she was standing in the doorway, waving her arm after him. He waved in turn. No doubt she could not see the gesture, but she would feel it.

26

THE MONSTER

HE TIED UP the gray mare five blocks from his destination. Walking was not too easy; his feet were cut more deeply than he had thought when he washed and bandaged them in the bathroom. But he made himself step out freely, lightly. He would be walking through fire, before this night was ended.

The face of One-hundred-and-twelve looked to him as before, but taller. Lights shone through some windows; the shades of other windows were illumined. There ought to have been more noise. The place should have been bursting with illumination; because inside that building, he was certain, were the Doctor and his men. They had reason to celebrate.

There was a narrow sidewalk lane that ran past the building. It clove clear through the block; a street light shone dimly at the other end.

He walked around the block and came in from the other side. When he reached the foot of One-hundred-and-twelve, he found the lower windows were clouded glass with wire frozen into the glass. They were well locked, of course.

He pulled his automatic, thrust the muzzle of it against

the top of the lower sash, and pushed. If he jerked the weight he was lifting, the sash might go up with a screech when the latch broke. He had to press steadily, exerting more and more pressure by degrees. He lifted until there was a shudder of effort in his right elbow and his legs had turned to stone with the strain.

The latch gave way with a brittle, crunching sound. He pocketed the automatic and lifted the lower sash. There was empty darkness inside. The darkness rolled out into his face as he leaned over the sill.

He stood back and glanced up and down the alley. No one was in sight. He looked up the wall of windows above him. No one was on watch.

The Doctor was a brainy man, but he was not using all his brains, this night. Perhaps he counted too much on past experience. Because experience teaches us that one beating a day is enough for a man; and on this day big John Witherby had been beaten once already.

Well, the Doctor might have a few things to learn before morning; otherwise, Witherby would be a dead man.

He slipped in over the sill, reached up, and closed the window behind him.

His feet did not touch the floor. He hung by his hands and still his feet did not touch the floor.

He pulled out the pocket torch; hanging by one hand, he slit the darkness with a few knife-like slashes of brightness. He was in a great boxlike room with a heap of litter in one corner, a jumble of second-hand furniture in the others. The walls were concrete all around. A stairway went up in a farther corner. The place was like a prison. The air in it was stale.

However, the drop to the floor was only four or five feet. He made the drop, cushioning the impact on tiptoe and loosened knees. The blow hurt the balls of his cut feet unmercifully.

He went up the stairs. They turned a corner, came to a door. The door was locked. It opened inward.

He went back to the heap of litter in a corner of the room below and found a stiff wire presently.

The end of the wire was too thick to work into the wards of the lock. He took the butt of his automatic and hammered the wire-end into a chisel. With that he started work again. He spent ten minutes. He began to sweat. This door might be the stopping of him before the night's work had begun—but just as he reached that thought, something gave. A moment more and he had the door ajar.

It opened on more blackness which he split with the light from his torch.

An infinity of danger still separated him from the Doctor. If he had used his brains, he would have finished off the Doctor that other day. Even if men charged instantly through four doors into the room, it would have been better that way. But how could he have told, on that day, that he was really talking to the devil incarnate?

The door had opened on a hall; he went down its length. It made a turn. There was glimmering of light. Another turn showed him a flight of stairs, narrow, with iron bindings on the edges to keep the stone from wearing away. These ought to be the back stairs of the building.

Floor by floor he mounted until he was on the fifth. That was the level of the Doctor's rooms. On that level extended the long, wide, well-furnished passageway with the soft

rugs on the floor. In that comfortable hall there were sure
to be watchers.

He opened the door at the landing. It showed him the
beginning of the hall which he had just been picturing.

He leaned. The first glimpse of his eye showed him
emptiness. There was a wild flurry of his heart. What if
fortune were to favor him and give him a chance to enter
a more intimate zone of danger?

In the distance, somewhere, happy voices were talking
and laughing. There must be liquor in there. People have
not that careless abandon of laughter unless there is liquor
around. Or were they drunk with money?

He stepped boldly out into the hall, closing the door
behind him, his right hand on the automatic in his pocket.

But the hall was empty! The fates had given him a golden
chance!

He moved a few tentative steps. Then a doorknob turned
with a click. A door down the hall jerked open, wavered.

A voice came out: "I'll tell him you're coming, eh? The
sucker will turn green when he hears—"

Witherby, desperate, half a second, half a step from being
discovered, jerked open the door beside him and stepped
into merciful blackness. He closed the door.

THERE WAS A sound of metal scratching on metal. A cone
of light sprang across the room, centered on him.

"Stick 'em up, brother," said a husky voice.

"What's the damned idea, anyway?" asked Witherby.

"The idea is heaving the hands up. Do it fast, stranger."

The last word was a blessing to the trembling soul
of Witherby.

"To hell with you," he said. "My assignment is this room. What are you doing in here? Who are you, anyway?"

"You don't know me, eh?"

"Why should I?"

"Yeah? Why should you? There's plenty of reasons why should you—if you're right. You belong, is what you mean?"

"Yeah, but do you?"

"Stick up your mitts, you fool, or I'll sure drill you!"

"I'll make a holler," said Witherby. "If you start anything the Doctor'll show you the lining of hell!"

"Turn on the light by the door," said the husky voice. "I'm gunna look into you, kid!"

Witherby reached out, swept the wall, found the switch and turned it. Light jumped through the room. Not from a central fixture, but from three floor lamps. Their pools of brilliance showed a davenport, two or three small tables, deep, easy chairs; their softer margins enabled Witherby to make out a pair of garish modern paintings on the wall.

He saw this setting, but above all he was seeing, in the greater dimness against the opposite wall, a vision that could have been fitted more easily into a nightmare. It was one of those gorilla types that are approximated, sometimes, by warriors of the ring. He was not much over middle height, but there must have been thirty pounds more than two hundred in the square bulk of him. Massive as he was, his hips pinched in sharply. His clothes were tailored to show off the smartness of this figure. He looked like a dressed-up monkey. He would not have had to lean far forward to walk on all fours.

And the face that went above the body matched it. Even if he shaved twice a day, there would always seem to be a

fur on his dark skin. The mouth was the worst part. The
lips were loose. They did not fit in against the teeth. When
he talked, the mouth kept unfurling in unexpected places.
Sometimes the lower lip hung down in the middle, and the
teeth appeared. They were irregular teeth. They seemed to
be worn down in front. The mouth was chiefly what one
saw in that face. There wasn't much chin. The eyes were set
under an outfold of the brow.

"My God," breathed Witherby. "You—"

The monster grinned.

"Seen me before?"

"No—"

"Yeah, but you heard them talk about me. They're always
talking about Shorty. And people can remember me—they
can see me by the talk."

He took a waddling step forward and rested a hand on
the table. The hair was thick on the back of it. The hair was
thick all the way down to the first joint. That hand gathered in a cigarette from an open box, took a match from a
smoking stand, lighted the smoke. The other hand kept an
automatic leveled. Separate intelligences governed those
hands. They could think for themselves.

The first shock was still echoing through the body
of Witherby. And doors seemed to be shutting, one after
another, in his brain, closing away the thunder of a great
report. He came back to himself by degrees.

He had been afraid of one brain in the world. That was
the Doctor's. Now he was afraid, physically, of the first
man he had ever seen. Professional boxers—they may be
dangerous if a fellow has to wear gloves against them. They
crumpled up if the grip of big John Witherby was clamped

on them. They were soft. This grotesque looked soft, too—like rubber.

"Now out with it. Who are you?"

"It's a surprise—seeing you, Shorty. I didn't know—"

"Didn't know I was around? Yeah, but I been around."

"The Doctor doesn't pull you out of the pack till he needs an ace," said Witherby.

Shorty shook his head. The movement was short, as though the neck did not allow much play.

"Why should he waste me?" he asked. And he grinned, as though his vanity had been touched again. The smile was uncertain. Smiling was not the thing to employ all of that mouth. Witherby could imagine another expression that would, and the thought made him weak.

"Let's hear more about you," said Shorty. "Seems like I've seen you somewhere before. Borneo, Singapore. Ever been in those parts?"

"No," said Witherby.

"Maybe I'm wrong. But I'm not likely to be wrong. I've seen you somewhere—doing something. Somewhere you wouldn't see me. I wonder."

"Well," said Witherby, "I'm glad that I've run into you—at last."

HE WENT TO a table, sat down in an easy chair.

"Yeah, you're all right, or else you're just cool," said Shorty. "But wait till I get my brain working, and remembering. If you been lying, I'll chaw you up."

He said it calmly, and took a great whiff of his cigarette. The strength of the draught made a length of the tobacco turn into a blazing coal, but the heat did not seem to bother Shorty. The smoke whirled in a great gust from his lips.

"What job are you on?" asked Shorty.

"You know—the Witherby thing."

"Same as me, eh? This Witherby—you ever seen him?"

"I've seen him, all right."

"How big is he?"

"Oh, about my size."

The little eyes of Shorty gleamed up and down.

"Yeah? That all?" he pondered.

"I'm pretty big," said Witherby.

Shorty laughed, and sat down. His feet did not reach
the floor. He wobbled them back and forth in an uncertain rhythm.

"Yeah," he said, still laughing, "you're pretty big."

He stretched out the fingers of the hand that held the
cigarette and closed them again. "Yeah, you're pretty big,"
he said. "Go on and tell me some more about Witherby.
What does he look like?"

"Not like much. Not much more than me."

"Then he don't look like much, all right," assented the
ape.

He laid the automatic on the table beside him. Witherby looked suddenly down at the floor. The game, he felt,
was in his hands.

"The chief wants me to get Witherby," he said. "He
wouldn't of brought me all the way in to town except for
that. He wants me to finish off Witherby that way—with
my hands!"

"You've done the same trick with others, they say," said
Witherby.

"The same trick? Who says I have?"

"Everybody says so."

"Yeah, and they better say so. All you gotta have is the hands to do it, and the trick's easy. There was a Nigger in Colon that come at me with a pick. I grabbed the pick with one hand, and I grabbed his throat with the other. He couldn't reach me. I held him out till he died on his feet. That takes a grip."

"And an arm, too," said Witherby, looking closely into the beastly face.

"This Witherby, they say that he's stronger than he looks. He bends iron, and things."

"Yes," said Witherby. "He bends iron, all right."

"What else does he do? Tear packs of cards?"

"Yes. Sometimes."

"Packs of cards, eh? How many? One?"

"Two packs."

"Hold on—two packs of cards?" said Shorty. "Wait a minute—now I remember—Singapore—that dive by the river—tearing up two packs of cards—by God, I knew I'd seen you before! And you—you're Witherby yourself!"

27

DUEL OF THE GIANTS

THE NERVES OF Witherby were alert; they had been drawn taut for many long seconds. Now he jumped the gun out of his pocket with a quick gesture. He was not any faster than the sudden grasp of Shorty.

Some miracle—or was it a flash of mutual recognition of danger?—kept them from firing. They sat still and stared at one another.

"What's the good?" asked Shorty. "If you plug me, I'll loose a ton of lead into you before I die. And the others, they'll come in and get you."

"Maybe," said Witherby. He stood up, very slowly.

"Don't try to slide out. I won't let you slide out, brother," said Shorty.

"I'm going to lock the door."

"Lock it and be damned. If you try to open it and jump outside, I'll nail you."

He did not try to open the door and jump outside. There were men out there in the hall. He could hear their voices, dimly. If he jumped outside, he would jump to his death, and he knew it.

But he turned the key in the door, for a new thought had come to him, a horrible temptation like that of jumping from a height. In the shoulders and the arms of Shorty there was more strength than he had ever seen in a human being before. Except, that image of himself which he had studied more than once in the mirror, wondering at the living slabs and lakes of muscles.

But big as the muscles were, they never fully explained the strength that resided in him. The quality seemed to be better than the quality of other men, In the same way, a cat is stronger than a dog. A hundred and fifty pound dog is a big clumsy brute. Strong, perhaps, but slow. A hundred and fifty pound cat is a leopard that would rip the hearts out of ten mastiffs in ten minutes.

And now, as John Witherby stood in front of the door, staring at the other man and his gun, the temptation burst upwards, like an exploding bomb. He had tried his strength against men more than once, but only when there were numbers. Otherwise, a shame held him back. He had never stood chest to chest with any man, and then put forth his entire strength.

He came closer to Shorty.

"What in hell's the matter with you, dummy?" asked Shorty. "You look like you were gunna slap my wrist, or something."

"The Nigger down there in Colon—how did he look to you when he was dying?" asked Witherby.

"Kind of funny. Why you ask? He stuck his tongue out. His face swelled up. He bit his tongue while it was sticking out. The blood started running down. He looked kind of funny."

"How would you like to see me look like that?"

"Maybe I will. There's something in my fingers that tells me I'm going to."

"There's something in mine, too," said Witherby.

"There's what in you?"

"Shorty, you never came anywhere near your match."

"God, ain't I been hungry to find a man that wouldn't just break up like matches!"

"I'm the man for you, Shorty."

"You? You ain't half big enough. Not a quarter!"

"Shorty, how would you like to carry me in over your arm and throw me down at the feet of the Doctor and say: 'Doctor, turn this over and look at it. Is this what you want?'"

"How would I like it? I *would* like it, and that's what I'd say, too. It ain't a bad idea—to say that—'turn this over and see if it's what you want'! That's great, Witherby."

"Suppose that we both put our guns on that table. Slowly. So there won't be any chance for one fellow to gyp the other. Then we'll have empty hands, Shorty."

"Well—my God, Witherby, are you really gunna give me my chance at you?"

"I've got to get out of this room, and I can't get out till you're dead, Shorty."

"Yeah, and that's a fact. One holler and I'd have the gang in on you."

"But you're a real man, Shorty. You'll keep your mouth shut and fight this out fair and square?"

"Will I keep my mouth shut? By God, I pretty near love you, Witherby, for giving me this chance. How'd you think of it?"

"It's a grand idea," said Witherby.

"When you look at me," said Shorty, with wonder in his voice, "don't you feel kind of sick and weak?"

"Not a bit."

"Well, damned if you ain't a halfwit, then, in spite of what they say about you."

"Do we put the guns on the table?"

"We do. Here's my start."

And with a perfectly frank and fearless gesture, Shorty laid his weapon on the table. After all, he had little to dread. Any loud sound would bring men to the door; and that door would be quickly smashed in.

Witherby passed the gun to his left hand and laid it on the table.

They stood before one another. Strength and a savage consciousness of it was swelling up in Witherby. And a foolish madness of joy was transforming the face of Shorty.

"We shake on it?" asked Witherby, holding out both hands.

"Shake? Yeah—just like the ring!" murmured the husky voice of Shorty.

And instantly his immense grasp was on the hands of Witherby. They stood straight.

IT HAD SEEMED to Witherby that he could never find flesh that would withstand the might of his grip. The bones of ordinary men crackled under it. But these huge, hairy fists did not give way. The blood compressed from the fingers of Witherby. Twice he thought that his hands were giving way. His arms were shuddering. Terrible doubt leaped up and choked him.

And then he saw that the arms of the gorilla were trembling, also. Perhaps the same wild doubt was in the soul of

Shorty. Aye, it was there in his face: horror, and amazement beyond speech.

For another long minute they retained their grips.

Then: "By God!" breathed Shorty.

"It's no good," said Witherby.

"We'll have to try another way."

They loosened their grasps and stared at one another. They were breathing hard. And each, as he looked on his equal, felt bewilderment and vast disbelief.

"I wouldn't think it. I wouldn't dream it," said Shorty.

A disdain rushed up in Witherby like a madness.

He held out his arms horizontally.

"You're beaten already, Shorty," he sneered. "Take the first hold—and carry on!"

Instantly Shorty lowered his head and swayed in. His great arms gripped the body of Witherby. The contraction pressed out the breath of Witherby. The knuckles of a great fist were grinding into his backbone and threatening to break it.

He thought, for a moment of blackly swirling dizziness, that he was gone. Then, flexing all his muscles, he made the constricting arms spread until he could breathe again.

He humped his back, reached far out, and joined his hands behind the back of Shorty. It was like pressing against slabs of hard rubber. He gave all his might to the effort—and the huge back of Shorty was still bowed out away from him.

In his own ribs there were growing aches. If one of those small arches of bone under the flesh gave way, others would follow. His side would smash in; he was sure of it.

And the entire force in his arms he gave vainly to the

effort to bring the back of Shorty straighter. They stood at a deadlock, each apparently matched in strength of arms as in strength of hands.

Then the legs of Witherby flew from under him and he fell on his face. Shorty, with the most ancient of wrestling devices, had gained the first good advantage in the bout. He used it to a deadly purpose, and before Witherby could turn, he found his neck gripped in the fork of Shorty's huge arm.

As if that strangling device were not enough, Shorty's other hand came over the face of Witherby to jerk his head back.

Witherby plucked that hand away; he jerked the arm straight. With a two-handed lock on the wrist he began to twist the flesh against the bone. Then the entire arm turned. Vainly Shorty strove to pull the arm free. Suddenly he gave himself to the bone-breaking grip and hurled himself over the shoulder of Witherby. The hold of each man was broken, and like fighting beasts they went for the throat.

The huge clamps of Shorty fastened around the neck of Witherby. His own clutch was on the rubbery neck of Shorty.

And Witherby, taking a deep breath, bowing his head, succeeded in forcing his chin down against the thumbs of Shorty; his own grip was well under the chin of the other, but he felt that he was squeezing a huge tire blown hard with compressed air.

HOLDING THAT GRIP they rose to their knees, to their feet. His head bowed against the hands of Shorty, Witherby could not see the fellow's face. But he could hear the strained breathing.

He worked his thumbs in jerks. At every jerk, the muscles distended to protect the vital windpipe from that crushing pressure. And Shorty, striving to use the same device of a pulsating grip, found himself hindered by the well-lowered chin of Witherby.

It seemed to Witherby that he was gripped by a shrinking collar of hot iron. Bands were working into his flesh, bruising it, working off the tender skin. The neck muscles, unused to the prolonged contraction, began to shudder and threatened to give way.

A heavy blow struck his leg. Another beat against his right thigh.

Shorty was kicking furiously to break from the position.

All weakness left Witherby, for he felt that that struggle on the part of Shorty meant that the huge fellow was giving way.

His bowed head enable him to look down. He saw one of Shorty's huge feet raised to kick, and he himself struck forward with the heel of his right shoe. He aimed at the shin bone and found it. The bone crunched like a rotten stick, and Shorty's weight lurched down.

His knee did not strike the ground, however. The mighty arms of Witherby prevented that, as they received the entire down-lurching weight. And the jerk, like that of a hangman's rope, drove his thumbs suddenly deep into the throat of Shorty.

A cry came out of Shorty's lips. It was the strangest sound, the most horrible utterance that Witherby ever heard. He could feel it bubbling deep in the neck, under the tips of his thumbs, which at the same instant thrust in deeper than ever.

He had throttled the cry. His own breath was being shut off. He was needing all the wind that could be pumped into him by a mighty bellow; and he had had to live on what he could get through an arrowing reed. But now the grip of Shorty was snatched away.

The huge hands of the monster began to beat like clubs at the head of Witherby. The shock of the blows knocked waves of red and black across his brain. But his thumbs were thrusting deeper and deeper. All his hands were sinking farther into flesh of a throat that was suddenly yielding.

There was a rap at the door.

When no answer came from the room, a voice could be heard, calling faintly: "What was that? Who sang out in there?"

Witherby could not respond. The voice was throttled in the windpipe of Shorty.

Twice more he beat heavily at the bowed head of Witherby. Then he relaxed.

And Witherby for the first time looked up.

The horrible picture that he saw made his hands release their grip instantly. Shorty, a loose, rolling, almost liquid weight, spilled forward, struck his shoulders against the knees of Witherby, and lay face downward on the floor.

He was dead. His brutal hands lay outstretched, the fingers still crooked as they had been to tear out the life of his enemy. There was no need to feel for the pulsation of his heart. He was dead. One look at the empurpled face, the thrusting tongue, the bulging eyes, had told Witherby the truth. He hoped never to see that picture again.

28

HANGING TO LIFE

FULL CONSCIOUSNESS CAME slowly back to him. The terrible strain through which he had just passed could not be called consciousness. It was nearer to a dream—except that a dead man now lay on the floor at the end of the nightmare.

And as his senses all came back to him, he was aware that hands were wrenching at the door, and a voice was saying: "Who's in there?"

"Shorty."

"Hey, Shorty."

"He's having one of his damned sulking fits."

"Not tonight. He knows the chief means business, tonight."

"What'll we do? Smash the door in?"

"No. Here's Mickey. He'll pick the lock."

"All right," said the voice of another—Mickey, perhaps. "We'll have it open in a jiffy."

"Shorty'll catch hell for this."

Shorty already had caught hell.

And Witherby ran to the window and looked out. The wall of the building leaned far down to the narrowing street beneath him. Some people were coming out of the restaurant on the corner. A woman in the party began to laugh—high, shrill, drunken laughter. It was closed away behind the door of a taxicab.

Witherby climbed through the window.

He had not thought of where he could flee. He only knew that to remain in the room would be death.

There was quite a wide, projecting sill, and that was one step towards fortune. It ran on past the margin of the window, so that he could stand clear of the glass. There were projecting eaves above the window, also. He reached up, and gripped the edge. With his left foot, softly, he pushed down the window.

Would they rush in and throw the window wide?

The door went open, inside the room, with a crash so distinct that he realized that he had not shoved the window down all the way.

"Holy hell!" yelled a man's voice. "Hey, Shorty! Shorty! *Shorty!*"

The same voice gasped, on a lower tone. "It ain't a game—it ain't a game—he's dead, or something."

"Turn him over."

"My God—look—at that—*face!*"

"I don't wanta look. Who said there ain't devils and a hell?"

"He's dead. He must of had some kind of a fit."

"Fit? Look at that throat! Look at the black places—look at the skin tore off—he's been strangled!"

"You're crazy! Not even a gorilla could of strangled Shorty!"

"Then it was done with a rope!"

"Rope my foot—hands have had hold of him. Hands have strangled him—"

"Witherby!" said someone.

"Witherby? He'd eat two like Witherby."

"You forget how Witherby went through us that night— all I got was the touch of his shoulder as he charged. It was like being grazed by the shoulder of a running horse. Witherby—by God, Witherby is here!"

There was a sudden stroke of silence.

Then: "Look behind that curtain."

"Look yourself! I don't wanta go probing for no damned gorilla like what choked Shorty."

"Yeah? You guys keep your guns on that curtain. Look close, will you? Hey!"

"That was only the wind. Go on."

"Keep your guns on it, for God's sake." Then: "No— nothing here."

"Behind the davenport!"

"Take it from both sides. You guys go that way."

Silence again, and: "Nothing here! Where could he be?"

They would be peering out the window before long, and what could Witherby do?

He looked desperately around him. Better a headlong dive into the pavement of the street below him than to fall into the hands of the men of the Doctor—or to yield to any death that the Doctor might select for him.

Well above the eaves of the window where he stood there was another projecting sill. For a fingerhold, the face of the building offered the crevices between widely spaced ornamental stonework. To climb such a perpendicular surface seemed impossible, but nothing is impossible to a desperate man.

Big John Witherby began to climb.

He kept his body well in, never bending his back out as he raised a leg. He turned his feet out, and made frog's-feet of them. With fingers of each hand he secured what hold he could, crooking the fingers at the ends.

If only the tremor would pass out of his body—that shaking which was the inevitable result of the terrible struggle with Shorty! But he felt the quaking all through him, and his nerves and his muscles would not be still.

He went up, a step at a time, a short, short step, a precarious step!

His feet mounted. His hands clawed like steel hooks on the stone crevices. Then his fingers could grip the sill of the window above, and his feet could stand on the projecting eaves over the window where he had just been standing.

Such a terrible, shuddering relief came over him that his knees almost gave way and spilled his body outwards. He looked down at the street at the same instant, and his nerve gave way utterly. In the whirling of his mind, he could not tell whether or not he was hurtling down through the bodiless air.

But his hands, thank God, were still clamped on the sill of the window above him.

THE WINDOW THROUGH which he had just come now dashed open.

"Nothing out here. How could there be?" said a voice, clear and ringing.

"Look up!"

Witherby saw the fuzzy top of a man's head.

"Nothing up there, either. Witherby ain't a fly, is he?"

"Boys, we gotta find him, or hell's to pay. The Doctor'll go nutty!"

"Call the Doctor now. This here thing has gone far enough. If we don't call him, he'll give us *more* hell."

"That's a true thing!"

The voices left the window.

They had gone for the Doctor, and when he came—

Witherby turned his face back to the wall, freshened his grip on the sill above him, and pulled himself up with the sheer strength of his arms—he dared not give himself the advantage of a leg-jump.

But as his head rose above the sill he saw—a blank wall. There was merely an ornamental indentation.

He stared at the margins of it. Perhaps there had once been a window planned or actually cut through, but now it was walled up—and that ended progress this way. For above that window projected the wide eaves of the building, and he knew that he could never reach out to them, loosing his hold on the wall, turning and springing up as he leaped. Not even a circus acrobat, trained to dizzy feats, would have attempted that trick, with a hard street pavement six stories beneath!

He lowered himself from the sill again, and stood on the eaves beneath, his head turned.

And at that moment a light flashed across him.

It cut back. It steadied. He waited for bullets to stream down the path of the light.

Then, turning his head as far as he could, almost at the risk of falling, he saw a boy at a window across the way—a boy with a strong pocket torch in his hand. Perhaps he had been amusing himself shining it down into the faces of people on the street. Chance and the devil had made him pick out the figure of Witherby.

The young fiend sat laughing in his window.

How call him off?

It is as vain to threaten a devil—or a boy—as it is to threaten a hawk in the sky.

So Witherby turned still more, precariously. There are no limits to a boy's ideas of games.

Witherby laughed. At least, he opened his mouth, and leaned back his head to give the semblance of hearty laughter. Then he pointed down at the window below him, and a moment later waved his hand in the universal signal of "No!" He followed that with the signal: "Get down!"

A lad does not need to be a boyscout to understand that signal. And the boy across the street, to the infinite relief of his victim, suddenly flashed off the torch and dropped down behind his window sill. He waved one assenting arm to Witherby, and then only the blond top of his head could be seen, glistening under the electric light of the room behind him.

At the same moment the voice of the Doctor sounded below Witherby.

29

THE NEXT JOB

HE COULD HEAR the testimony.

"We heard a kind of a yap, in the room, here."

"No, it wasn't no yap. It was a sort of a holler and a groan, all mixed up."

"And you broke open the door at once?" said the cool, distant voice of the Doctor.

"We hollered, first. There wasn't any answer."

"And then you broke down the door?" demanded the Doctor, his voice a little louder.

"Along come Mickey, just then. We knew that he could pick the lock. We knew that you didn't like to have things messed up around here—"

"You waited, did you? You fools!"

"Chief, it was only a minute—"

"An automobile can go a mile and a half in a minute."

Then, from the Doctor: "Shorty's gone, eh? Strangled. I suppose—outside of a zoo—only one pair of hands could have done that trick. Witherby's been in here."

"That's what we kind of thought—we looked all over the room—"

"Before calling me, eh?"

"If we could get him cold for you, chief—"

"My God, what sort of men have I working for me?" exclaimed the Doctor.

His voice sounded at the window. It rang, almost, in the very ear of Witherby.

"That other gun—there are two guns on the table," said the Doctor. "This has been a pleasant little duel. They put their guns aside and settled the affair with their hands. Yes, I can recognize Witherby in this."

Then: "Bring me a pocket torch."

A slight click of metal on metal. A pause.

"No—no sign here that I can make out," said the Doctor. "When you came in, what about the window?"

"Closed."

"Closed down tight?"

"Yes, down tight."

"That's strange," said the Doctor. "A man working for his life would hardly stop to close the window after him—but that fellow Witherby—"

His voice changed, rose, swelled: "By God, I could drink hot blood when I think of him! You looked down the side of the building?"

"Aye, and there wasn't a thing."

"We looked up, too," said another.

"Did you think that he was a fly, to walk up the face of the stone wall?" sneered the Doctor. "But how could he have gotten down, leaving no sign? Nothing fastened here—not the end of a rope—nothing?"

"Not a damn thing, chief."

"The answer is that he didn't leave by the window. Have you sounded the alarm?"

"Yes, sir. There's men on watch at every door, down there,

and walking the beat around the building. There goes one of our men, right now—around the corner."

"Then he's here in the building," said the Doctor. "We know that much, to begin with. He's here in the building, and he'll be dead when he leaves it."

"In an ashcan—that's how most of him'll leave it!" said the voice of Charlie.

"Ah, you're here, Charlie?" murmured the Doctor. "I'm glad you've come. I need you for a little procedure that ought to start now."

"Where?" asked Charlie.

"In this room. Before it begins, start two squads of men rummaging through the building. One floor at a time. Open every door—to every room and every closet. Start at the bottom and go on to the roof. You understand?"

"All right, chief."

"Tell the men that Witherby is in the building. Tell them that I expect to have him here inside of half an hour. If they miss him—but they won't miss him!"

Footfalls sounded.

The voice of the Doctor sounded, barely audible: "Once I had men—now these!"

Only a few minutes passed. Then the voice of Charlie: "I've started them. And they're ready for his blood, chief. They want to know one other thing—when the split comes."

"What split?"

"The Finley cash."

"Who wanted to know when the split would come?"

"I forget. Several of 'em."

"Try to remember who they were."

"All of 'em are talking about it, chief."

"Are you one of the all?"

"Me? I'm not such a fool. But we've got a lot of green men."

"Tonight's the proof of that. I'm going to take a tighter hold, Charlie. I've been a lamb with them. I've been a woolly lamb. But by God, the time has come when I'm going to shut down on them and show them a master."

"I don't blame you," said Charlie.

"Don't whine, when you agree with me. If you don't agree, say so!"

"What I was thinking—it's a lot of money. It's the biggest lot of money that ever came the way of the gang."

"You know it's nowhere near what we expected."

"I know that."

"You helped me count it, didn't you?"

"I helped you count. But even eight hundred thousand is a hell of a lot of money, chief."

"Aye, to some people. If it had been the two million—if it had been that—why—it would have meant something to me. It would have meant something to you, Charlie, too."

"Thanks, chief."

"But as it is, we have to carry on at the old hangout."

"IT'S A GOOD lay, anyway," said Charlie.

"It's a fair enough lay. But it's going to cost more and more. That damned district attorney—he's raising his prices."

"What's the matter with the fool?"

"Witherby went to see him."

"I knew that. But Witherby didn't stay half a minute."

"That was long enough. When a lion looks at a dog,

one glance is enough. The rat is shaking in his boots. He's afraid of an investigation—he's afraid—ah, I don't know what he's afraid of. Witherby is the answer to everything that's in his mind."

"I'll have to go down and talk to him."

"Leave him alone. Too many of you fellows have been talking without my orders."

"Not me, chief."

"Stop whining, I tell you. Charlie, you're only half the man you were. I see that something's gone out of you."

"Anybody but you, and I'd croak them before I'd let 'em say that!"

"That's better. That's more like it. Now we'll get along to the other thing."

"Ready for anything, chief."

"You think you are, but maybe you'll change your mind before you're through with the next job."

"Try me."

"Go get Cherry, and bring her in here."

"Wait a minute, chief."

"What's the matter?"

"You forgot—the stiff's in here."

"I haven't forgot anything."

"Want me to throw a cloth over his face?"

"No."

"Bring the girl in—and let her see it?"

"That's what I told you."

There was a brief pause.

"I hope I get this right," said the voice of Charlie. "I'm to bring the kid right in here—and let her see Shorty— like this?"

"She may see more than that, before I'm through with her."

"Cherry? Has she gone wrong?"

"What in hell's the matter with you?" demanded the Doctor. "You're full of nothing but questions, tonight. I never saw anything like you!"

"Sorry," said Charlie. "I'll go get her."

"And when you see her, keep your mouth shut. Don't tell her that there's anything in here except me. Come along with her, and let her take the looks of Shorty cold. Here—help me sit him up in that chair against the wall."

There were scuffling, dragging sounds.

"What a weight of a man that is!" gasped Charlie.

"Beef—beef—beef," said the Doctor. "Too many pounds of beef, and he trusted to his head instead of to his hands. All of these strong men do that."

"Except Witherby," said Charlie.

"Damn Witherby!" exclaimed the Doctor. "I've heard enough of him—and he'll be hearing enough of me, in a half hour or so when I have him in here."

"Have you got an idea for him?"

The Doctor laughed, broodingly, happily.

"I've got an idea," he said, "that'll please even you, Charlie."

"Paint his face like Shorty's and you'll be doing a trick."

"Before Witherby dies," said the Doctor, "Shorty's mug is going to look like a study for a singing angel. I've been thinking about Mr. Witherby almost since I met him, and now I think I have the sort of an idea that's worthy of him. Now get along and bring the girl to me."

Footfalls retreated. The door shut. Then came a sound of

slow pacing. Eventually the Doctor began to whistle, and that was what big John Witherby wanted.

To climb had been difficult. To descend would be twice as hard. But he worked his way down until his hand was on the eaves where he had been standing.

After that, it was simple to lower himself softly to the sill of the room where the Doctor was still pacing back and forth.

He ventured to take hold of the edge of the lower sash. In that way he lowered himself still more until he was sitting on the sill. His position, now, was much safer, in spite of the dangling legs. He was at ease, and above all, he could both see and hear whatever happened inside the room.

30

"DEAD AS FISH!"

TAKING IT ALL in all, it was the most brutal device that Witherby had ever heard of—this bringing of a young girl into a room where a corpse lolled in a chair against the wall. And what a corpse! The look that had sickened and blinded Witherby was still on the face. The contortion had not slackened. As in the last instant of life, so in death the mask was frozen with perfect horror. The head lolled over on the vast shoulder. One glance, and Witherby felt that it was wiser to look no more.

The door opened. The girl appeared, with the tall, thin form of Charlie behind her.

"Hello, Doctor. Want me?" she said, brightly.

Then she saw Shorty.

She made no outcry. There was simply a wrinkling of her face in distaste. Then she walked across the floor and stared at the monster closely.

"So that's the end of little Shorty, is it?" she said. "The poor dumb baboon!"

The Doctor was staring; so was Charlie.

"What did him in?" asked the girl, still looking at the corpse.

"Bullet, I guess," suggested the Doctor.

"Men don't look like that when they're eating lead," she answered. "Try another. A rope, maybe."

She bent and peered more closely.

"Or hands," she said.

"You mean to say that hands could do that to Shorty?" said the Doctor.

"Some hands," said the girl.

"What ones?" asked Charlie.

"You know what ones. Witherby's." She turned abruptly on them.

"What sort of a game is this, Doctor?" she asked.

"I'm wondering how you could guess that Witherby did it. It was done right here. It was done right in this building. It was done in this room!" said the Doctor.

"Then Witherby must have been here," she answered.

"Then Witherby's a dead man," said the Doctor.

"He's been dead for a long time," she said.

"Dead?"

"Yes, ever since he started bucking this game."

The Doctor made a pace or two back and forth. The girl squinted at Charlie. He shrugged his shoulders imperceptibly.

"I won't need you, Charlie," said the Doctor.

Charlie went to the door.

"I'll be standing by," he said.

Then he went out, closing the door with much precaution behind him.

"What's the idea?" asked the girl.

"I'm going to find out," said the Doctor.

"What?"

"What's in your head."

"Not much," she replied.

"Plenty!" he answered. "There's plenty inside that head of yours. Cherry, answer up bright and brisk."

"Fire away."

"You love John Witherby!"

She was silent. A queer shock ran through Witherby. He could not breathe.

He wanted her—no matter what the consequences— he wanted her to cry out in a great voice: "Yes—yes, yes! I love John Witherby!"

But the Doctor had to exclaimed: "Answer me!"

"You poor fish!" said Cherry Larue.

And then she laughed. Her laughter was as honest as any that Witherby had ever heard. It broke off in the middle.

"What are you trying for?" she asked.

"The truth," said the Doctor. "And I know the truth. You love John Witherby."

"Oh, I do, eh?"

"Sit down."

"I'll take this standing."

"Just as you please."

"Are you trying to rat me?"

"You love John Witherby. You helped him find the Finley money."

"I told you about that. I told you how I ran into him in the woods. What else was I to do except to follow along?"

"You saw him tie up Sexton."

"He tied Sexton before I bumped into him."

"That's a lie."

"Ah, Doctor," said the girl, "what a gentleman you are—

and what a penetrating intellect! What a brain—to feed to fish!"

He sighed.

He took out a cigarette, rapped it on a thumbnail, lighted it. As he blew smoke into the air, with a toss of his ugly head, he still was watching her, carefully.

"You were with Witherby, and you gave him the steer about the graves."

"Did I?"

"He hasn't the brains to figure out a thing like that."

"How do I know who figured the thing out? Maybe the old hen at the farm house did his thinking for him—he did his own digging, is all I know."

"You could have brought Ad and Charlie to the spot with even a whisper, when they went by."

"My whisper would have been the last one out of my lovely lips," sneered the girl. "That ham-handed bozo would have broken my neck the first sound I made. He had his big mitt on the back of my neck when the boys with the lights went by."

The Doctor hesitated. Then he shook his head.

"Too many features that all hang together," he said. "You lead him to the stuff. You go away with him. You run like hell to keep up with him when we get on the trail. And you stand on the bank and wait for him when he heaves over the top of the hill."

"What was I to do?"

"Buck into the brush, I suppose."

"Yes, if I wanted to get away from you—not if I wanted to get away from him."

"You stood out there as a last play, ready to go with him

if he could get back to you in time with the boat. Then, when we came up, you pretended that you were with us all the time."

"LISTEN, DOCTOR," SAID the girl. "I hate to argue with you when your brain's asleep, this way. But I'll tell you something. Suppose that when I bumped into him I'd managed to get away—suppose I hadn't gone alone willingly with him—well, wouldn't he be safe at home, now, with eight hundred grand in his Christmas stocking?"

The Doctor shook his long head again. From the back, it looked like the head of a boy.

"It won't do," he said.

"Cook it some more, then?" suggested the girl.

"Cherry, you're a bright girl, but this won't pass."

"Doctor, you're a bright fellow—when you're awake."

"You also engineered the chance for Witherby to get into this building."

"What a girl *I* turned out to be," scoffed Cherry Larue.

"You passed him the word that told him when he could safely cross the hall and get into this room."

"Turned him right in where he could be clubby with the pet boa constrictor, did I? What a loving lover *I* am."

"Don't talk like this, any more. It's not your natural way of speaking, Cherry. And I don't want any more of it."

"What's my natural way of speaking, papa?"

"You know, perfectly well. This pretense—this affected hardness isn't any part of you. You're not out of the slums!"

"Only now and then," she answered.

"Ah? Such as when?"

"When I have to talk to half-witted old bozos that try to read Cherry's mind."

"By God, Cherry," said the Doctor, "I've made up my mind—"

"Try the garrote," said the girl. "It's a neat way of passing out down the same road with Shorty. Maybe I can overtake him if you give me a boost along the way."

"Cherry," said the Doctor, "I like to listen to your chatter. But under the chatter, there's a vein of danger in you. The fact is, my dear, that you are only half a step from death just now."

"Am I?" said the girl. "What a two-faced liar you are, dear Doctor! But you can't bluff me."

"Bluff you? Bluff you?" exclaimed the Doctor. "Do you think—"

"No, I don't think that a woman is a whit safer with you than a man is. But this murder talk is bluff. That's why you wanted to talk to me in the room with poor little Harry, yonder. Bluff, dear Doctor."

"Are you sure, my dear?" he asked her, with a frightful smile.

"Perfectly certain. The emotions don't rule you, old son. I mean too much money in your pocket. You mean too much money in mine. And there you are. You're a hard man, Doctor—you're, a clever man—and what you lack in cleverness you make up in organization. You and I are the sort that ought to team together. We *have* to team together. But let's stop this silly bluffing game."

"Cherry," said the Doctor, "I'm sorry. I'm afraid that I've been making a fool of myself."

"How long is it since you've been in love?" asked Cherry.

"Eight years—ten years."

"Then it's ten years since you've made a fool of yourself.

You haven't made a fool of yourself tonight. You've only been a little hard on the nerves."

"Nerves?" chuckled the Doctor. "You haven't any nerves, my dear."

"I have, though," she said. "I'm really glad this nonsense is ended—and I don't like to have Shorty staring through my backbone. I'll leave, if you don't mind."

"Just a minute," said the Doctor. "Now that I see how you really stand with Witherby, I have some news for you, Cherry."

"Have you? Real news? Cherry hasn't had any real news for these many days."

"It won't mean as much to you as it means to me. But— congratulate me, Cherry!"

"Tell me—about what, papa?"

"I saw him only ten minutes ago. There's still a glow in me. He's dead, Cherry. Those bright eyes of his are as dead as fish. Those hands of his are limp as rags."

"Dead? Who's dead?" she asked.

"John Witherby," said the Doctor.

Her head went back and her hands went up. "No!" she cried. "No! No! No!"

She had a screaming voice, but the sound it made was no bigger than a whisper.

31

BEHIND THE FLAP

THE VERY GESTURE of grief and despair was hardly made before Cherry Larue straightened herself with a jerk and gasped: "You lied!"

"Too late, Cherry!" said the Doctor.

It *was* too late. She had shown enough of her true self. A flash is enough to show us the greatest mountain, from head to foot. And all her pretense of devotion to the Doctor, all the reality of her love for Witherby had appeared in that instant.

She realized it and ran suddenly for the table where the guns lay. But the Doctor was nearer; his stride was longer; the automatics were swept away from under the reaching hands of the girl.

She stood panting by the table, staring.

"Poor Cherry!" said the Doctor. But he spoke through his teeth.

"Well?" she demanded.

"We'll have to see," he answered. "I have to wait a bit and recover from the shock of surprise. The bewilderment, Cherry, now that I realize that you could lose your head about such a thick-handed and thick-witted slug as Witherby. Poor Cherry! And what a beautiful career I intended for you! What a blaze of glory for Cherry Larue!"

She had been very pale, so that her eyes looked huge and dark. Now her color began to return. There was a deep well of courage in her; she was drawing on it now.

"Whatever you do for me, it'll be something worth while," she told the Doctor.

"The pity of it is," said he, "that so many of the boys have felt that I've been favoring you unduly. There has been a good deal of jealousy of Cherry Larue. Now I'll want some of the boys to sit in at the session when you come up for review, Cherry. You won't mind that, will you?"

He laughed, cheerfully. He rubbed his long, lean hands together and drew in his breath as though the air were water.

"All right," said Cherry Larue. "I'll take what's coming to me."

"Ah, you think so—but you can't be quite sure," said the Doctor. "There are some things that even a Cherry Larue would hardly expect."

"What do you mean by that?" she asked him.

He merely smiled and shook his head. "We'll have to see. I have some rough men working for me, Cherry. When they learn that you've betrayed us and worked with Witherby, I wonder what they'll feel and what they'll wish to do."

She watched him with the groping air of one who is striving to get past an outer wall at an inner and hidden meaning.

"I'll trust to luck—and the other men," she said.

The Doctor snatched up the suitcase, then he turned for the kill

"Why not trust something to Witherby?" asked the Doctor.

He could not even wait for her answer, because a hard, cold rage mastered him and made him cry out: "He'll be in this room before another five minutes. Do you know that? He's in this building, and I'm combing it from top to bottom. He'll be here. I told you he was dead. Not a fact of the moment, but a fact that you can see accomplished. Here—in this room—with your own eyes! You understand?"

A light flashed across Witherby and over the face of the window. The infernal boy across the street was sweeping him with the powerful electric torch again.

"What the devil is that?" exclaimed the Doctor, and strode to the window.

He stood within half-arm distance of Witherby. One grasp and the Doctor would be helpless in that great clutch.

But Witherby did not stir. The boy at the opposite window had disappeared.

"Something from a passing car, perhaps," said the Doctor, and turned back to Cherry.

There was a rap on the door; the voice of Charlie sounded outside it, on a note of alarm.

"Come in!" called the Doctor.

Charlie entered with a quick, soft, sidelong step.

"They've searched the building from the basement to the attic," he said. "There's nothing!"

"Nothing? There's Witherby, I tell you!" said the Doctor.

"They've gone over every inch of the place."

"Great God!" cried the leader. "D'you mean to tell me that the fellow can turn himself into thin air?"

"There's only one other out—it wasn't John Witherby that killed Shorty."

"**LOOK AT HIM** lying there in the chair. Look at the finger-marks on his throat. Tell me any other man in the world who could have done that to him! Who but Witherby?"

"Aye, but even Witherby couldn't have mastered Shorty in a fair fight," said Charlie, shaking his head.

"What do you make out of it, then? One of my men? What one of them could have managed it? Their hair stood on end every time that Shorty's name was mentioned. They wouldn't dare to lay a hand on him!"

"Not one of them, maybe. Two, perhaps."

"What the devil would they stand to win by murdering Shorty?"

"Don't know. I'm just telling you that we've combed every inch of this building, and Witherby isn't inside it. That's the fact."

The Doctor pulled out a handkerchief, mopped his face, and cast a worried glance over his shoulder.

"It's the queerest thing that ever happened to me!" he declared.

"A lot of queer things have happened ever since we ran into this Witherby," answered Charlie, shaking his head.

"Queer? Yes, too damned queer. Where are the men who searched the place?"

"Outside in the hall."

"I'll go talk to them."

"Just a minute, chief."

"Are you going to give me some more gratuitous advice?" snarled the Doctor.

"I'm trying to tell you something that's worth knowing. Those fellows, out there—they—"

He paused. The Doctor glared at him.

"Go on, Charlie. Talk it out. Don't mind the little beauty in here. She doesn't count from now on."

"They're afraid, chief. They've got a panic in them. They know what Shorty was. They feel sure that nobody but Witherby would have had a chance to kill him in a hand to hand fight. Now Witherby has puffed out like a breath of smoke and dissolved into thin air. It makes them nervous. They're a jumpy crew just now."

"I'll soothe 'em!" said the Doctor, through his teeth. "Come on with me and see what I have to say to 'em!"

"I'd go easy," said Charlie. "If you call them yellow dogs, it may put their backs up."

The Doctor glared at his lieutenant, and strode from the room without another word. Charlie shrugged his shoulders, hesitated, then followed his master into the hall.

The girl, when she was alone, dropped into a chair. She leaned over the table with her face in her arms. The straight of her back bowed. Strength to resist had at last gone out of her.

AND IT WAS now that Witherby at last slipped through the window. There was no safety in entering the building, but he could not stay much longer on a ledge outside the place. He made little noise as he glided over the sill, under the raised sash.

It could not have been more than a whisper the girl heard, but it was enough to bring her out of her chair with a gasp. She was standing, a picture of horror, when he straightened.

"Go back!" she breathed, making a frantic gesture with both hands. "John, John, go back the way you came—the Doctor's coming back in an instant—and men with him—go away—quick!"

He went up to her with an unhurried step.

"How about you, Cherry?" he asked her. "Are you safe in this place?"

"Of course I'm safe!"

"The Doctor doesn't suspect a thing?"

"Not a thing. He thinks I'm a genius—he claims that the gang owes the haul of the Finley money to me. I'm ace high, and perfectly safe. Only—get yourself away, John!"

He listened to the lies with a sudden twisting of his heart.

"I'm not a bird," he said. "I can't get away, out there. But I've been on the window sill all the time the Doctor was with you. I know how safe you are in his hands, now."

"He's only talking," she began. "He won't do anything—"

He took her face between his hands and leaned down over her.

"My God," said Witherby, "what a small lot of you there is! And what you mean to me!"

"Do you really mean that you can't get away?" she asked. "You can't leave by that window—just as you entered?"

"No. There's no way. I've got to come in, sooner or later."

"We *have* to be together, then?"

"We do," said Witherby.

She sighed out a great breath of relief.

"Then nothing matters," she said. "The Doctor will kill us, John. You know that?"

"I suppose so. Damn him—I may be able to get my hands on him first—"

"Have you a gun?"

"No, but have you?"

"Nothing! John, they'll mow us down. We only have half a minute, perhaps."

"I want you to tell me who you are, and where you came from, and how you happened to be with the Doctor—" he began.

"That would waste time. I'll tell you only this. I've only been a silly girl, so far—not a bad one. The first time I tried to do a really bad thing, I met you. That's all the time we'll give the past. It's this minute that counts. It's loving each other that matters. And if—"

The voice of the Doctor, high pitched, harsh, metallic, sounded down the hall, dimly, as he approached the door.

"Here!" said the girl, breaking off suddenly. "This would cover you both, John. Look!"

She snatched from the foot of the davenport a big, soft,

knitted throw of tan wool. This she flung over the horrible figure of Shorty.

"Behind it, John!" she whispered. "Quickly. You can hide there. Behind Shorty, with part of the throw over you. You can wait there—"

"Wait in a hole while you face the music?"

She pushed at him with both hands. She might as well have striven to move a rooted rock.

"But then you'll have a chance to do something—surprise will make you into ten men, perhaps. It's our only ghost of a hope—"

He saw that she was right. But already the knob of the door was rattling as he sank down behind the screening figure of Shorty, and the girl threw a flap of the woolen cover over him.

32

KILLERS' JURY

THE DOCTOR CAME in first, carrying a suitcase, and behind him walked eleven men, of whom Charlie was the last.

"Sit down where you can find places, men," said the Doctor.

They sat down here and there, in chairs, on the overstuffed arms of the davenport, and two or three had to remain standing, or pacing nervously here and there.

"You've covered up Shorty, eh? Get on your nerves?" asked the Doctor.

"It got on my nerves," said the girl.

"Maybe you'll get something more on your nerves," suggested the Doctor.

There was a long fringe hanging from one edge of the woolen throw. Through that fringe, Witherby could see most of the room and all of the faces except that of the girl. She sat in a straight backed chair, turned away from him, and he regarded her judges with a dying hope.

The Doctor had not called in all his men. He had selected the chosen hands, and well-tempered evil had hardened every face. They were not old. In years, not one of them had seen more than thirty, but experience had worked them over with hammer and chisel until the surfaces were all the same.

There was as much difference between them and other men as there is between dogs that have run wild, making their living by wits and teeth, and dull-eyed pets in a house.

Witherby had been in many parts of the world, but he felt that in all of his travels he had not seen another twelve men like this jury which was about to sit on the case of Cherry Larue. What their judgment would be, he had no doubt. Sympathy for her because she was a girl and beautiful would not enter their minds.

And when the judgment was given—well, he would find something to do. He could, at least, charge out at them and go down in the fight.

The Doctor opened the proceedings by putting the suitcase on the table.

"Here's the Finley money," he said. "We'll make the split of it before we finish this session. We'll dispose of the girl, first."

There was cunning in that sort of procedure. These fellows would not let their judgment linger too long on the case of Cherry. The matter of the hard cash was more important. They would brush her aside to get at their rewards.

The Doctor opened the suitcase. Pack after pack of money appeared, greenbacks in stiff, brown-paper wrappers. There was a little stir among the judges. Their eyes left Cherry and settled fixedly on the treasure.

The Doctor said: "Charlie, I think you know this case. What have you to say?"

Charlie screened his lank face behind a cloud of cigarette smoke. When he spoke, his breath knocked holes in the cloud.

"We're a chain," he said. "That's what we are. If we hold together, we can lift a lot of weight. If one link breaks, we're no damned good. Cherry's the link that broke."

No one said anything in comment. But several of the men nodded their heads.

"Is that all you have to say, Charlie?" asked the Doctor.

"That's all that needs to be said," he answered.

"State the case to 'em."

"Why, the case is dead easy. Cherry says she met Witherby in the woods, and that she made up with him again, and that he took her along and let her watch him find the stuff. That's the bunk. You can see what the fact is. She's double-crossed him three times, he thought. Would he let her do that again? No, not unless she could pay her way.

"And she paid it, all right. She'd worked out the meaning of that thing that stumped us—the cross over the nine. The cross stood for a grave. Mighty clever! A thick head like Witherby's would never have worked out that puzzle. So she took him to the spot. Why? Partly because she was batty about him. Partly because she knew that if we got the dough she'd only get a small split. If Witherby got it, she'd have all she wanted. A two-way split. Isn't that clear?

"When we chased Witherby with the dogs, she was running with him, wasn't she? She was waiting for him on the edge of the river, and the dough was with her. She pretended that she had played his game only because that was the only way she could keep close to the Finley money and throw it our way in the wind-up. But that's a plain lie."

"**MAYBE IT'S A** lie," said the husky voice of Ad, "but it ain't so plain."

Witherby was amazed. He had not expected Ad to be a supporter of the girl in this time of crisis.

"Why isn't it plain?" asked the Doctor. "Shall I make it plainer?"

"Go ahead," said Ad.

"Look at other things that have happened," said the Doctor. "Look at this!"

He stepped to the chair which was covered by the throw and lifted an edge of the cloth. Witherby, expecting instant discovery, gathered himself for a leap. But the whole cloth was not raised. The Doctor moved it only enough, apparently, to reveal the distorted face of the dead man.

"Have all you boys seen this?" asked the Doctor.

Some of the men got up and came closer.

"He swallered a lot of death before it gagged him," said one.

Another man remarked: "He got a pain in the belly before he finished his laugh."

"What was *he* doing with his hands? That's what beats me," said Ad.

"What does anyone know?" answered the Doctor, replacing the throw and stepping back to the others. "The point is that Shorty was one of the best men we had. When dirty work had to be done, Shorty was the only fellow of the lot who really enjoyed it. He snuffed out a life as willingly as any of the rest of you would snuff out a light. Now he's gone. He's been worth half a million to us, in his day. And he's never cost more than thirty or forty a week. Well, Shorty is gone. And what took him away from us?"

"Witherby," said Ad. "That skunk of a Witherby must of done it. Nobody else had the grip."

"Then how did Witherby get into the house?" asked the Doctor.

"I dunno. How did he get out, either?"

"A mystery, isn't it?" sneered the Doctor. "Go a little further into that mystery. In this house there's nearly a million dollars to be split up by the partners. Outside of the house there's a man who knows that the money is here. He wants to get it. He has the nerve to try it. To walk into a house filled with his enemies, where every man knows his face. What man would that be?"

"Witherby," said Charlie.

"This damned Witherby," went on the Doctor, "has the nerve to do almost anything, but he hasn't the nerve to do this, and he hasn't the ability to do this. He can't appear and disappear by magic. No, only with the aid of a friend inside the house. Who is that friend? The girl—there! I've just managed to trick her into the admission. She's confessed to me that she loves Witherby! Will you deny that now, Cherry?"

"Not if it would save my neck," said the girl.

"Good girl!" exclaimed the Doctor, relieved. "There's that much honesty in you. Now, then, my friends—is it clear to you? Witherby's girl is in the house. She gets him in. He happens to run into Shorty by surprise, where Shorty is supposed to be waiting in this room, and the room is dark. They fight it out. Shorty is strangled. And the girl manages to get Witherby away from the building again."

"How?" asked Ad.

"How do I know? A traitor can find a thousand ways of

doing things. The fact is that it was done. Witherby is safely away. God knows what trouble he's cooking up for us. We may have government agents and officers surrounding the place at this minute. And that we'll owe to Witherby—and what we owe to Witherby, we owe to the girl!"

"Damn her!" snarled Charlie. He added: "Do we vote on her living or dying?"

"Aye, vote," called one. And get her done with!"

"WAIT A MINUTE," interrupted the red-headed Ad. "I'd like to know if she don't get a chance to talk for herself before she goes under?"

"There's a fine legal spirit working in you, Ad," said the Doctor. "But—"

"I don't want to talk," said the girl, composedly. "Talking won't do any good. A crowd like you fellows, bound together to kill or be killed—why, you have reason enough to wish me dead, I suppose. I'll tell you some of the rest. The morning you got at John Witherby by moonlight— well, you thought that I walked him out into the trap, but you're wrong. I went out there to warn him, and get him away from the trouble—but I was too slow, and you were there too fast for me. And every other time I was always trying to help him, and always failing."

"She's talking it right out," said Ad. "I like that way of talking. Doctor, what's the harm in turning her loose?"

"No particular harm," said the Doctor. "She knows most of our secrets, of course, and she'll take them to the police, too. But I suppose that there's no particular harm. Some of us may get away from hanging, after she's turned loose. But what do our necks count, compared with life and happiness for a treacherous, pretty little rat like her?"

"There's going to be no more damn foolishness," said Charlie. "We'll vote, now. Those in favor of bumping off Cherry Larue, keep sitting. Those the other way, stand up."

Ad stood up.

Charlie turned around and snapped his fingers at Cherry Larue.

"You're dead, beautiful," he said.

"Thanks, Charlie," said the girl.

"You thought you were butting in and getting to be the queen of the hive. All you catch in the end is hell," said Charlie savagely.

A big block of a fellow with a handsome, brutal face leaned from his chair to snarl: "You turned me down. I wasn't good enough to sit next to you. Now you get this—and I'm damned glad of it."

"I'm sorry, Cherry," said big Ad.

"It won't last long," she answered. "Thanks, Ad."

"I suggest that we leave Cherry to the light touch of the chief," said Charlie. "Anybody vote against that?" There was silence.

"All right, Doctor. She's yours," said Charlie.

33

MUTINY

WITHERBY PRESSED HIS eyes closer to the fringe and saw the Doctor turn his long, pale face towards the girl with an air of infinite satisfaction, a slowly dawning smile that cast a slow wrinkle up into his forehead.

"Presently, Cherry," he said, "I'll attend to you!"

And she said nothing. Witherby could only see that she had turned her head and tilted it a little, so as to meet the gaze of the Doctor steadily.

"Before I take the lady away," said the Doctor, "we'll proceed to the division of the Finley money. Every man who has a claim to a share in the loot is here present. The girl's claim, of course, is gone. Our usual system is the one we should follow, of course. Fifty per cent to the house and the rest divided equally."

This speech was greeted by a silence. Darkly the men looked at one another. Then Ad said: "That means that you get eleven times as much as I get, Doctor."

"Maybe my work was worth eleven times as much," said the Doctor. "Charlie, what do you say to that?"

But Charlie muttered: "I was just thinking about that."

Red-headed Ad stood out from the rest; the eyes of the gangsters dwelt with a scowling intensity upon him. The

Doctor, folding his arms, dropped his head on his chest and stared up at Ad from under straight-ruled brows.

"You were only thinking, Charlie?" said the Doctor, softly.

Charlie said nothing.

"Suppose that everybody got an even split out of that coin. It would mean nearly seventy thousand bucks apiece. Suppose we all trim that off. We each give ten thousand to the chief. That makes about a hundred and eighty thousand for you, Doctor. It leaves less than sixty thousand for each of us. That pays you three times as much. It looks square to me."

There was not a murmur from the others. They simply shifted their looks from Ad to the Doctor, and waited.

The Doctor walked up and down the room a few times.

Then he said: "I planned the job. I discovered that old Daniel Finley had a ton of money hidden out. I discovered that he had sent for a nephew. I planned the blocking of the nephew. I sent a pretender out to get at the coin peacefully while we were putting Witherby—damn his heart!—out of the way. I located the riddle on the tape. I was the one who sat out on the hillside. When Partridge failed and was kicked out of the Finley house by Witherby, I was the one who put the bullet through the window into Daniel Finley so that he couldn't tell his nephew where to pick up the treasure. That gave us an even break. Then I arranged to kill Witherby and steal the tape measure at the same time. We missed on Witherby, but we got the tape. We would have won all the way around—except that there was a traitor with us.

"After I've done all of this, you want to cut me off with

less than a half share! Ad, I don't believe it of you! I've always marked you down as one of the most promising of the lot. And now you want to treat me like this? I'm surprised. I'm ashamed of you, Ad."

It was a good speech, Witherby thought and a convincing one. Only at the end there was a touch of sentimentality that did not ring exactly true.

And Ad, settling on that point in the speech alone, bawled out, suddenly: "Yeah, like a father you love me, I'll bet!"

And laughter snickered, then rolled out in broad thunder.

The mockery struck the Doctor like a knife. He jerked about suddenly and stared at the others. And under his eye a wave of silence succeeded the uproar. They sat tensely again, staring at him. And the beast was in every eye.

"I've been hoping," said the Doctor, "that you'd all realize that there are other anxieties that go with the leadership of an organization such as this. There are the lean days, when nothing comes out of the pot. There are all the men who have to be hired and fired at the bottom of every job. There's police protection that has to be paid for. All of these items come out of my share. I suppose none of you think of this?"

Silence greeted this appeal.

Ad said: "What has anybody ever got out of the gang? Is there a single gent that ever backed out and was able to settle down and enjoy the coin that he'd been working for? Who knows about anyone who ever got more than a bullet through the head, at the end of his trail with the Doctor."

"Not a damned one!" exclaimed Charlie, suddenly.

"ARE YOU SAYING this, Charlie?" asked the Doctor, and his voice was a gentle and a deadly poison.

"It's the truth!" said Charlie. "I never thought of it, before."

"Do you fellows think that I've been growing rich?" cried the Doctor, suddenly beating on the table.

"If you're not rich, then the whole business is a farce and a fake," declared Charlie. "We've been carrying on all of this time with no real chance to collect. All we've had out of the thing has been money enough for a few trips and a few drinks. Average life of a fellow in this gang is about two and a half years. That's the fact of the matter. Doctor, the time's come to split up this coin and call the game off!"

There was an instant murmur of agreement. The Doctor looked around in a white, still passion of rage. Then, to the astonishment of Witherby, he nodded his head.

"In a case like this," said the Doctor, "it's always my custom to allow the majority to rule. I'm sorry to hear this decision. But I can't say that I'm frightfully surprised. Not a very great deal surprised. I've felt a growing opposition in the gang. And, since you are all united, there is only one thing for a wise man to do—bow as gracefully as possible to necessity."

He passed out of the view of Witherby.

A moment later there was the sound of the door opening and shutting.

Ad stood a commanding figure by the table.

"If I had my say," he declared, "we'd make it a straight split all around. We'd slice this into twelve parts and call it a go! We'd each have a stake that would be worth while."

"Right!" snapped the incisive voice of Charlie. "Remember this—he'll never forget and he'll never forgive us. By God, if we use sense, we'll only split this deal into *eleven* parts. We won't give him a hand. That'll pay him back once for the thousand times that he's crooked us. He won't hate us much more than he hates us now, at that!"

"What did he mean by slipping away, like that?" asked Ad. "Was he too damned choked to talk any more?"

"He wanted to take it out on the girl—God help her!" said one man.

And Witherby, looking towards the chair where she had been sitting, saw that she was gone!

34

THE DEATH BANDAGE

SHE MUST HAVE gone without a word, quietly submitting to the gesture of the Doctor which bade her follow.

She was gone—and she was gone to death by some horrible contriving of the Doctor!

Witherby stood up. The throw fell away from him. He stood with a contorted face before the men.

He heard the slight groan of fear and astonishment. He saw the flash of the guns that covered him. He was a dead man, of course. But that method of dying was utterly painless. It was nothing compared with the agony to which the girl had gone.

What could he do?

He wanted to dash for the door, burst it open, rush into the hall—but he would not dream where the Doctor had gone, and he would fall riddled with bullets before he took a step.

He wanted to burst into a frantic appeal to their manhood to rescue the girl from death.

But no appeal to manhood would move those faces which now leered at him behind the guns.

What could he do to stir them?

And every second that passed was beating out death, death, death for Cherry.

"Here's a kind of an unexpected visit, Witherby," said Charlie. "I guess that you couldn't hold back when you saw us about to deal out your deck?"

He picked up a couple of the packets of greenbacks, as he spoke, and dropped them carelessly back into the pile.

"Call the Doctor back," said someone. "He oughta have a chance to see this. He's been thirsting for this for a long time."

"Wait a minute," said another. "This here is the miracle-worker. This is the gent that can turn himself into thin air. Where's the miracle now, Witherby? Let's see you work, boy! Blow out the lights and fly through the window, or something. We're all waiting."

"Yeah, call the Doctor!" said someone.

Then a thought rushed like a trampling of horses through the brain of big John Witherby.

The Doctor had gone too readily, too easily—leaving a vast fortune in hard cash on the table. It was impossible that he could have left the room with this pile of wealth lying loose. And yet he was not here. He had taken the girl—and gone. He had taken her as though revenge was far more beautiful to him than money. And yet that could not be true.

"Call the Doctor," said Witherby, "but he won't come back. He won't hear you."

"What's the meaning of that?" demanded Charlie.

"Don't listen to him," said one of the men—that fellow with the brutally handsome face. "What are you trying to do, Charlie? Give him a chance to talk his way out?"

"Let him talk his way out of this," said another, and deliberately raised his gun to take aim at Witherby's head.

The bright gleam of the gun-barrel, the high light on it steadying to a single point of flame, was nothing, not even a gesture in the eye of Witherby. For the girl was yonder—somewhere behind the walls. And what was happening to her?

"I mean that the Doctor won't come back because there's nothing in here that he wants!" exclaimed Witherby. And, as he spoke, the surety came over him. A great fortune in hard cash seemed to lie on the table, but it must be an illusion.

"What's the meaning of that?" asked one of the men. "Nothing for him to come back to? My God, there's almost a million for him to come back to—to look at, anyway."

"A million what? A million fakes!" cried Witherby. "A million phony dollars. A million in the queer. A million in counterfeit!"

The light on the leveled automatic wavered. The gun dropped. Charlie, with a faint moan in his throat, snatched up a pack of the money, ripped the brown wrapper away, took the top bill—for twenty dollars—up between his eyes and a light. Two or three others were doing the same thing, and their reports came in a rapid fire.

"A fake!"

"A sell!"

"He's done us in!"

That was the meaning of the comparative calm of the Doctor. He had judged beforehand that this prize would be too great for the integrity of his men. He had known that they would try to get the money into their own pockets. What he had exposed to them when he was trying the depth of their zeal, as he was convincing himself of their crookedness, was simply worthless woodpulp. Now he had gone, taking with him the real money, and leaving the girl dead behind him—

"Do you hear, boys?" cried Witherby. "He's got the money. He's murdering Cherry Larue now. Go fast—go on the jump and we'll get him, and God knows that I'll be with you to the finish. Will you take me along?"

Take him? Use him as a weapon against the devil in the Doctor?

They welcomed him with a single great shout. Then they rushed for the door.

They seemed to know where they would find the Doctor. Where they paused, with Charlie in the lead, it seemed to Witherby that there was no door at all. It was only a panel in the hallway. But on this, as the others stood hushed along the rug, Charlie tapped. Witherby was already up, at the shoulder of the leader.

In answer to the tap, a strained voice answered, inside the room: "Yes, yes? What is it?"

"I've brought you an answer, chief," said Charlie. "Better than you expect."

Over their heads, a brilliant light suddenly flashed and died. There was no other answer from the Doctor. And Charlie exclaimed at the same moment: "He's spotted us. He's seen us, boy. Get down that door!"

Three swift bullets from an automatic smashed the lock. The shoulder of Witherby dashed the door open, and he came staggering into view of great, terrible eyes staring at him—the eyes of Cherry Larue above the tight bandages which covered her nose and mouth. The closeness of the pressure made her skin purple. She was lashed into a chair hand and foot. The device of the Doctor was perfectly simple, perfectly characteristic. He would murder her without sound, and stand over her, reading the progress of the death in her eyes!

THE BANDAGES PARTED like rotten leaves under the fingers of Witherby. He swept them from her head, from her arms and ankles. And she was able to breathe great gasping breaths.

He hardly regarded what the other men were doing. He only knew that the Doctor had not been in view when he entered. For the rest, he was on his knees before Cherry Larue, and seeing nothing but the flush and struggle of returning life in her face.

The other men were busy enough, however. They had rushed through the room—it seemed a sort of a business place to the eye of Witherby, with steel filing cabinets banked along the walls—and they were battering now at the door in the rear of the place.

The shots with which they battered the lock were only gradually effective, however. By the ringing impacts, it was plain that the door was steel, and heavy steel. And Cherry Larue was on her feet before the door suddenly was beaten open.

The whole mob of the gang rushed through the doorway and their descending footfalls raised thunder from a flight of stairs. Witherby would have run in pursuit, now that the girl was back on her feet, but she kept him from following.

"You can't overtake him. He has two minutes start!" she panted. "John, how did you get here?"

"By walking out on them and showing them the stuff the Doctor had left was counterfeit. Come on, Cherry. I'm going to get you out of this—and then I'll find the Doctor somewhere—if I have to jump off the edge of the horizon."

"Hurrying won't do the thing," said Cherry Larue. "We've got to think—we've got to get out of here first—and then thinking is the only thing that will beat the Doctor!"

Which way should they go out?

They went straight back up the hall and down the main stairs. There was not a soul. The uproar which they could hear dimly in the distant and lower part of One-hundred-and-twelve was still rumbling, and no doubt the confusion had called every man to the spot. There was no elevator boy—there were none of those lounging rascals in the lower hall.

And they walked out onto the street together. It was empty, half-lighted.

Not a sound reached them from the interior of the Doctor's stronghold. It held up its blank, forbidding face exactly like its neighbors up and down the street.

They got into a taxicab at the corner.

"Drive slow!" said Witherby. "Drive anywhere—slow."

35

RACE FOR LIFE

SHE LAY BACK in the hollow of Witherby's great arm. And slowly the taxi crept down the street. Thin bars of light came through the windows from the street lamps and showed her to him. He had to drag his mind away from her.

"The Doctor!" he said. "He can't be the winner!"

"Which way will he go?" asked the girl.

She sat up, intent, suddenly on the problem.

"He'll head for the railroad station."

"Not in this town. That's the first place some of his men will go. They mean murder if they see him, John."

"They'll never see him, then. They're not the cut to get rid of a fellow like the Doctor. Bigger hunters will have to get at him."

"A railroad. That's the way to move fast."

"What about an airplane?"

"There's no landing field near."

"Is there another railroad anywhere near?"

"Ten miles across country."

"Well, he could go for that. What road—"

"There's no road that heads for it. Not one. It lies beyond the big hills—"

"Then he won't try to get to it."

"I don't know," said Cherry. "He has horses. He had sense enough to mount his men for the Finley job. Wouldn't he use a horse?"

"To cover the ten miles?"

"Yes. He could make that."

"Does he know the country?"

"If he goes out past the Finley house, he'll know it almost all the way."

"That's the thing he'll do, then," said Witherby. "You've hit on it! And by God, if he's on the way now, the gray mare may run him down for me."

"Is she with you?"

"Yes. She's—wait a minute, driver. Turn right at the next corner."

"John, are you going to leave me?"

"I've got to."

"Not now, when I'm still touching life—and not believing in it."

"We've got time for me to hear about the Doctor. If he used his time, I should have found you dead, Cherry."

"He wasted a minute or two. He was asking me if I could chuck the idea of you, and go with him. He was telling me that he had the whole Finley fortune in a suitcase."

"And you told him that you'd go, Cherry. You weren't fool enough—"

"He asked me to swear that I'd stay with him through thick and thin. Maybe I'm a fool. I couldn't swear and then break my word."

"Of course not—not you. Even if you knew—"

"When I wouldn't promise him, he went devil again. He gagged me first. I tried to make a fight of it, but he's steel.

I was like a baby. He tied me into the chair. 'I wish that Witherby could have a chance to see you here,' he said. That was all. Then he stood over me after he'd pulled the bandage tight around my mouth and nose. His eyes were smiling. He was devouring my pain. I kept from struggling. I looked down so that he couldn't enjoy my dying.' And my lungs were on fire—then there was that tap on the door. He turned a switch of some sort, and looked into a little glass affair on the wall. He said: 'My God—Witherby!' He snatched up his suitcase. There was yelling outside the door. He pulled a gun and turned on me. Someone shot through the door. Maybe the bullet grazed the Doctor, otherwise, I'm sure he would have shot me. But he had to think about his own safety. And he went through the end door of the room. Then all of you broke in—"

They had turned the corner to the right, and in the near distance they saw the gray mare, standing with head down, patient, at a post.

When Witherby left the taxi, Cherry Larue followed him, tugging at his sleeve.

"If you go against him you'll die, John!" she pleaded. "No one has ever beaten the Doctor. When he shoots, he never misses. Even if you're unlucky enough to sight him, you'll be a dead man, John—please don't go!"

He stripped her hands away from him, kissed her, lifted her back into the taxi.

"Keep this machine," he commanded. "Go out with it to the Finley place. Tell Lizzie Finley what I'm doing. D'you hear? Go in there and talk to her. If I have luck, I'll be at the house before long—before more than a couple of hours,

I hope. I'll ride straight through across the hills and try to sight the first train that goes up the track."

He slammed the door over her protest and her reaching hands, and sprang into the saddle on the gray mare.

But Cherry had surrendered. The taxi started away. He could see the pale waving of her hand at the rear glass of the car. Then he turned the head of the mare and trotted her down the street.

THE BEAT OF the hoofs raised gigantic echoes, like iron beating on iron. Down the cross streets the echoes flew far away. Inside the blocks they rang back at him monstrously.

The houses thinned. He saw darkness past the lighted streets of the town. No, it was not darkness, but the even, white sheen of moonlight.

Then he was in the rocky fields. He reached a lane. It carried him a good distance in the right direction. He left it when it swerved to the right and took the mare steadily across country again. He wanted to ride her at full speed but that would be witless; for if chance brought him on the traces of the Doctor, he would find that gentleman well mounted, to be sure.

He began to remember strange, detached things— pictures of adventure far away—and then the first note of Cherry's song at Kelcy's—Uncle Daniel writhing on the floor, writing his incomplete message in his own blood—

Something rang dim and hollow and far away.

He stared through the moonshine. The air was misty and the moonlight was therefore dim. Yet by the ghostly light he saw the pale glistening of wood well over to his right, and out of that wood he saw a shadowy horseman pass.

He would not believe his eyes. He felt, first, a shock of

cold fear. As though he were seeing a phantom horseman! Then he called softly to the mare as, once again, the other horse rang a faint chime of her shod hoof against a stone.

He got the mare into her full racing stride. Almost instantly the stranger was bending low over the neck of his mount—a tall, thin rider, a tall, long-legged horse.

A fence rose—another—another—the gray mare was doing her best, but still the fugitive held his full advantage, a good field away!

36

A FOX IS CORNERED

WHEN CHERRY LARUE paid the taxi man and tipped him generously at the Finley house, she went around to the only lighted window.

She found herself looking into a kitchen where the tall, angular form of Lizzie Finley sat in a rocking chair, asleep, beside the kitchen stove.

Without knocking, Cherry opened the door and entered. When she turned from closing the door, she found the old woman sitting erect, with a big poker in her grip. The poker had a crooked jag in the middle.

They stared at one another for an instant, before Cherry could speak.

"I was told—" she began.

"You're my boy's girl, ain't you?" asked Lizzie Finley.

Cherry blinked, and then she understood.

"Yes," she said.

"What are you doin' out here at this time of morning?" asked Lizzie Finley.

"John sent me," said the girl.

"He didn't send you to stand around on your hind legs like a ninny," said Miss Finley. "Set down, here. Wait till I wake up the fire."

She put more wood into the fire box. The flames began to roar. Then she put coffee and cold water into a blackened pot.

She took off a small lid over the fire and put the coffee pot on the blaze. The drops of water on the outside of the pot ran down and hissed against the hot iron.

"You've got a pretty face," said Lizzie Finley, "but God knows what's behind it. Why did John send you out here?"

"To wait for him," said Cherry Larue.

"Is he going to marry you?"

"I hope so," said Cherry.

"You don't care much?"

"I want to see him alive—that's all I hope," said Cherry.

"What's the young fool doing?"

"Hunting for the worst devil on this earth."

"Aye, and he would be. And still hunting for the money?"

"Yes."

"He'll get it," said Lizzie Finley. "He'll get it if he has to die for it. The Finleys do the things that they set out to do. Who are you?"

"Cherry Larue."

"Stage name?"

"No."

"It sounds too good to be true," said Lizzie Finley. "But you *look* too good to be true. You love John?"

"Yes," said the girl.

"So do I," said Lizzie Finley. She put back her head and smiled a little, dreamily. "I never had such a big feeder eat after my cooking," she said, as though explaining.

But Cherry Larue had closed her eyes. Pain of fear, for an instant, was blinding her. Lizzie Finley began to exam-

ine the beauty of Cherry with the calm but searching eye
of a connoisseur. And the dreamy smile lingered on the
older woman's lined face.

The blaze roared up the stovepipe with more rapid vibra-
tions, filling the pipe with the tumult and the fullness of
the flame.

FAR ACROSS THE countryside, John Witherby was racing
the gray mare fast over the fences. And before him, he had
at last the joy of seeing the other horse come back to him,
not steadily, but by slow degrees.

At the second fence beyond, the fugitive turned his
head suddenly, and gave a long look behind. After that he
crouched low over the neck of his horse and urged it to a
greater speed.

But it was a dying spurt. The long, raking stride of the
mare was telling. Again she began to gain, and this time
rapidly.

It was the Doctor. For a long time, Witherby had been
practically certain. Now he was close enough and the moon
was bright enough for him to identify the spare, long form.

The Doctor turned. A gun flashed in a wide arc in his
hand. He fired. A humming sound jumped close past the
ear of Witherby.

And he remembered what the girl had said about the
shooting of the Doctor.

For his own part, he had a good loaded automatic in the
case which was strapped behind his saddle. He pulled it
out, now, slid back the safety catch, and kept the gun ready
as the mare gained.

They were straining up an easy, long slope, now, with
the boarded windows of an old farmhouse showing to

the right. This one, at least, had not yet been reoccupied. Perhaps it did not belong to the estate of old Finley. And yet they must be close to that familiar ground.

Once more the Doctor turned, fired. The report of Witherby's own gun chimed on the heels of the other. Pain streaked the left side of Witherby. Burning agony tormented the nerves.

But he called to the mare with a gasping voice, and she answered, unreeling some hidden energy so that she began to walk up on the Doctor hand over hand.

Witherby felt his side. It was wet and warm with blood. But the bullet had merely ripped open the flesh on the outside of his ribs. It was a scratch, in his reckoning.

The Doctor was swinging his horse to the right. Witherby turned the mare to take the hypotenuse of the triangle thus made. Was the Doctor quite mad?

Again the leader turned in the saddle. He fired not once but three times in rapid succession. There were whirring sounds over the head, past the shoulder of Witherby, and then a slashing wound across his left thigh.

His teeth set over the burn of the pain; he put into an answering shot. He could not have the least idea as to his accuracy, but he knew that his steady hand was trying to counteract the wavering movement of the gallop of the gray mare.

Now he could understand the move of the Doctor. He was going to dodge around the empty house—he was going to try to get away into the woods behind it.

Now, in fact, the pursued disappeared around the corner of the building. And Witherby, with the savagery of a hunting hound in his heart and between his teeth, shot the gray in pursuit.

As he rounded the rear of the dwelling, he heard galloping hoofs among the trees. He was about to spur in pursuit when, through a gap in the trees, he clearly saw by the moonlight the silhouette of the other horse, running on with an empty saddle.

Had the Doctor fallen wounded from the saddle? No, that was unlikely.

John Witherby pulled the mare to the right again, and sweeping up behind the farmhouse, he was in time to see the dark mouth of a door shutting in the white wall of the building.

The fox had taken to ground!

37

THE END OF THE CHASE

SPEED WAS THE thing. To get at the man before he was well lodged in a safe spot—Witherby gave the door his shoulder and the stout wood flung him back.

He took the width of the porch and ran low, bunching his weight behind the padded muscle of his right shoulder. The door went down with a crash. He rolled headlong.

From above, a light fanned down on him. He had a glimpse of a narrow hall, a flimsy stairs climbing the side of the wall. And above the light came the barking of a gun, through the light came a stream of bullets.

Why should not the Doctor have planned to take advantage of just such a bull-rush, such a blindly stupid attack as this?

John Witherby got to his hands. A bullet through the left shoulder knocked him down again. He lay on his wounded shoulder and fired up under the light.

The torch snapped off. Through the darkness he heard running feet.

He got up, unsteadily. The drain of blood from three wounds was sapping his strength; the pain made him dizzy. His left arm hung dangling, senseless at his side. Perhaps it would be useless forever.

But that did not matter. If he could get at the Doctor with one hand, it would be enough.

He ran up the stairs, unlimbering his own flash light. Perhaps it was madness to run through darkness with a flashlight instead of a gun in his hand. But he could not hold both, and the first necessity was to see his way.

Through the little bedrooms he blundered. Twice he came to locked doors. They went down in splinters before his charge. He made the round of the entire upper part of the house. There was no trace of the Doctor.

He found the ladder into the attic. That would be the place!

Gingerly he pushed the light before him over the edge of the trapdoor, then swept the dusty emptiness with the torch. But there was no sign of the Doctor.

He returned to the head of the stairs.

Perhaps the Doctor was out of the house, now. He might have doubled back past his pursuer and vanished.

Down the stairs, Witherby shone the light and saw the red drip and gleam of blood on the steps. His own blood— or was some of the Doctor's blended with it?

He looked down on his own body. The left side was a mass of crimson. His clothes were soaked with his blood.

And, as he stood there, uncertain, he heard out of the distance a very light, rapid, crackling sound. The thing bothered him. It came from the right of the house, and down on the first floor.

So he descended the stairs again and turned to the right, through the unfurnished, dusty waste of a dining room.

He could hear the crackling more clearly now. A light seemed to be shining behind a door. He switched off his torch to make sure and in fact he saw a red line of light etched irregularly around the edge of the door. The crackling increased. He knew, suddenly, without the smell of smoke, that it was fire.

And his mind spun at the thought.

He tried the knob of the door. It was locked. He wrenched at it. A bullet split the door and hissed past his face.

The stroke of his right shoulder sent the door down, shattering. Again the gun spoke; and again the bullet missed.

He had dropped the torch back into his pocket because he would not need its light in there. He had the automatic ready as he charged.

And now he saw, in the farther corner, head and shoulders propped against the wall, gun steadied across a raised knee, the Doctor himself, lighted by the flames which rose from a tangle of old newspapers that had been piled against the wall. The flames were already racing up the wall, and curling out across the flat of the ceiling above. And, in the middle of the flame, there was a heap of compact parcels of greenbacks, each held firm by a brown paper wrapper.

He saw these things with a single sweeping glance—a tenth of a second of seeing before he smashed a bullet straight into the body of the Doctor.

He saw the long form jerk over on one side. The legs snapped up, and the head of the Doctor bowed down over his knees. That convulsive movement had sent the gun of the wounded man slithering across the floor.

Even the Doctor was a secondary consideration then. Into the fire leaped Witherby. It was impossible to stop it. The flames had too deep a rootage in the dry wall, but they had not yet burned more than the outside edges of the greenback packages, stacked like compact little bricks. Witherby kicked that treasure into the clear. The empty canvas sack from which they had been poured was close at hand. Into it he swept the money again. And the fire was roaring, spreading, turning the room into a hot oven before he strode to the Doctor.

The latter, like a crushed worm, had been dragging his body towards the spot where his gun had slid. He turned over on his side as the foot of Witherby kicked the automatic away.

He had been struck twice by the fire of Witherby. And both bullets had drilled through his body. Perhaps the dizzy agony was already commencing in the Doctor before he turned for the deserted farmhouse. Undoubtedly one of the bullets had been that which Witherby fired while he was lying prone on the floor of the hall. But either shot would have accounted for the life of the Doctor.

He gripped at the wounds with one hand. He tried to speak. Only a spray of blood left his lips. He made another effort.

"Cherry—" he managed to gasp.

That was the end. He dropped without a struggle and lay with his head on his arm.

The flames had eaten already through the side wall and permitted a powerful draft to sweep into the room, driving great streams of fire across the doorway.

It was dangerous enough for Witherby to get himself through the passage without trying to lift the body of the dead man.

Besides, was it not better for even the body of the Doctor to vanish utterly from the earth?

With head bowed, Witherby caught up the canvas sack and charged through the doorway. As he gained the hall he looked back into the red mouth of an inferno. A whistling draft was at work. It made a singing sound that sickened the heart of Witherby.

OUTSIDE HE SAW that he could do little or nothing with his wounds. But the Finley house could not be far away, and the mare would find it, perhaps. She would know where to go if he let the reins hang slack.

He tied the canvas sack behind the saddle and mounted. He was dizzy—very dizzy.

He had to keep his place by maintaining a firm grip on the pommel of the saddle. And the mare broke into a dog trot as though she knew perfectly that her rider was no longer the strong man.

From the top of the first hill he looked back. Straight streams of fire were rushing up from the burning house. The glow of it seemed to streak the horizon with rose. Or was that the coming of the dawn? The mare went on steadily. Waves of darkness began to come at him from a distance and break across his brain.

HE MIGHT HAVE been sitting the saddle for ten minutes in front of the kitchen door of the Finley house before the mare pawed impatiently at the wall.

Lizzie Finley it was who threw the door open and saw by the morning light a horseman adrip with blood which had run down over the gray hide of the mare also.

She had to shake the arm of Witherby. She had to shout at him thrice before understanding came into his glazing eyes. Then he slid to the ground and stalked with sagging knees into the kitchen.

Cherry Larue was beside him. His right arm dangled over her shoulders. She was holding up a great part of his weight. He felt the weariness of a man who must fall asleep at once. But he knew that beyond the sleep there was to be a wakening into a beautiful life.

"He's bled enough to kill a horse, I suppose," said Lizzie Finley in a calm voice. "But he ain't been touched in the vitals. My cooking'll put him on his feet inside of two weeks."

He knew it was true. The face of Lizzie Finley wavered drunkenly before his eyes. The only sure, steadfast and unchangeable fact in the world was the girl who walked beside him.

She would be beside him forever.

He could see, with his dim eyes, that he had reached the end of the trail of adventure and come to the peace of a perfect happiness.

Lizzie went before, pulling chairs out of the way, and Cherry, with her slim, warm arms, helped him over the threshold of old Daniel Finley's room.

www.ingramcontent.com/pod-product-compliance
Lightning Source LLC
Chambersburg PA
CBHW070221030726
47505CB00006B/1757